The
Living god

The
Living god

Sam Heaps

ΣΆΡΚΑ

*As the windows were smashed by
the ringing of revolution.
Down on our knees we're begging you please,
We're sorry for the way you were driven.*

—Phil Ochs

6 A.M.

In the dream, Jesse was a woman.

I like that, I tell him.

Jesse curls inwards, shaking his head against my body, "No you don't."

I stroke the length of his neck and croon, Shhh.

Jesse's skin is sticky with cold sweat. Lint from the hotel blankets. Waking, he usually lies silent beside me until I compel him to move—eyes closed, tracing the long scar which runs down the middle of his chest and then forks beneath each pectoral like a cross.

This woman Jesse who reaches for me as he wakes is pawing, twitching. On his side like this he exposes to me the right corner of his jaw which wears heat blisters.

My fingers almost touch the wounds, pry them open again.

I say, Jesse. I say, Jesse, tell me about the dream.

Jesse speaks through my side to the center of my stomach where our child is sleeping.

Jesse says, "In the dream I was—"

He stutters, so stops.

I am used to an internal thrust, or a compression, when Jesse is close to me. But, this morning there is nothing.

Jesse tries to start again, "In the dream—"

He stutters and stops again.

Jesse, raising his face to mine, "Touch me?"

My hand rests on Jesse's chest and upper shoulder, then I move it down towards his cock.

Jesse, "Not there." Jesse moves my hand to his stomach and presses himself against it while he closes his eyes, afraid to see my reaction. But I do not pull away. I keep the right palm where he has planted it, and with my left, cup beneath one breast like it is heavy. Jesse sighs with relief.

Jesse tries again to explain the dream to my torso. "A big voice was holding peaches while others were freezing—," "My body made food why wouldn't—," "My husband—I—"

I have never seen Jesse so soft.

I allow the change to drape over us, unsure if it will make intimacy's transformative qualities too visible and cause Jesse to run from its danger.

The spirits have commentary.

I believe the spirits are a gift from Elaina. Our beloved. Our prophet. If I were to share with her this belief with her, though, she would laugh and tell me I ascribe her control over every aspect of my life in order to avoid accountability. Elaina would insist that if I feel trapped by these voices, it is a consequence of my own passivity. My own longing for domination. Elaina would tell me that the spirits are just my mind's inventions, addled as it is by want without her presence.

This thinking also causes the spirits to snicker.

They are right, Elaina liked to lie.

The spirits are distracted though. They have tales of their own griefs and betrayals which they demand I hear, and hear *now*. Their volume only adds to the intensity of my ruminations, my desire for Jesse to leave his dream and return to waking life. Also, my desire for Elaina's touch this morning. Her demanding pressing limbs, her form to rise to, to meet. If only the spirits would shut up. Their stories are too numerous at this hour to discern one from the other anyways.

Jesse, "In the dream, you were singing."

I pretend when Jesse tells me this I do not see a flash of Elaina's strong brow running left and right over the top of my knee as she hummed, then stopped. Her eyes jolting beneath their lids with sudden violent thought.

The spirits, Look at us. I swat at them.

I wrap Jesse in the hotel's pilled yellow blanket and remind him I do not have the voice for song. Jesse grabs my wrists like he is drowning, his palms cold and wet from the night's terrors.

Jesse finally demands, "Why?"

I am not so stupid, I hear what is beneath the question. The years of unrequited need, layering, calcifying into hatred. His judgment. His mistrust. Our family. Elaina's body. And, most intensely, Immanuel.

In the parking lot outside the motel a truck backs into a parking space. A man talks into his radio. A tree in the window assigns purpose to acquired nutrition. Will grow.

The spirits of the uncountable thousands of bodies who have been here in this bed before us burrow into the sheets one on top of another on top of another on top of another. A woman too proud to beg for it details the actions as they could occur. She is stoic, like Elaina. Legs crossed.

A spirit is jerking off in the corner, pants around his thighs, back turned to us on the bed.

A spirit is reciting Hamlet's final lines to Ophelia.

A spirit with an exposed breast is praying to Jesus Christ for a pillow to latch.

The motel room is sour with our mortality. Jesse's musk smeared in all the towels. The combined odor of our shits and our morning breath and yesterday's coffee grounds.

The child.

On the compound we spent our last summer with Elaina in the light of the sun god, running barefoot through the fields. Elaina laughed at our flesh which drank the gift of the sky. *My little playthings.* And we held her child up to the light to show all. *Immanuel,* the followers cried. *My man Manny,* I would whisper in his ear, and together we would giggle. There was singing by the fire. Warm limbs. Feasting.

Now we are so deep in the dark that despite the morning birds' acknowledgment of the beginning day, the sun still will not rise. But, I am grateful it is midwinter. The few hours of light in the afternoon exaggerate the grief which rattles in me like an apocalypse.

A spirit who lit a bank on fire sneezes, and I startle.

A storm begins to rage outside the motel window, the wrong season for it. It furies like an early August deluge. I try to soothe myself with the sound of the burden of water upon the windows. I remind myself rain brings growth. Water brings life. But I can hear the spirits around me whispering in conspiracy, in contempt of living. They say, Look at me.

The Elaina in my mind says, Now who do they remind you of, baby?

The Elaina I have carried with me, Is this what you wanted baby?

My Elaina says, Immanuel is waiting for you to come home.

Jesse is still talking slowly, pawing at my body. I say his name. I will pull him from this sleep. I say, Jesse, look at me.

The whites of his brown eyes are shot with red, like a mad horse. Like maybe he is asking to be put out of this misery. Jesse says, "Baby—your hand."

I had, in my own dreamy memory, slipped it inside the front elastic of his boxers, waking him.

Jesse, knuckles white around my wrists, "Why would you not let me see Zion?"

Before the compound, before even the West. Back in the city in Elaina's ex-husband's Brooklyn brownstone, Elaina and I watched together a gathering of ants as they devoured a larger insect. The more massive body lumbered along a wooden plank as it was overtaken by what seemed to be a thousand little pinpricks. We could not see between them, they were stacked that tight and deep. We could not access the carnage. The show.

I said aloud to Elaina as we watched, What a horror we all are. What a horrible thing life is to have been brought to this world. It is cruel to each of us, all of these opposing wills.

Elaina then turned to me, her silhouette sunken and black against midday light, and she told me, *Baby girl, no*. Elaina told me what we had just witnessed was something beautiful, the power of shared intention, the sacrificing of the self for the community which was itself a godlike power. She gestured at the massacre, *See, the solitary are punished justly.*

I asked, Where do you draw your lines? How

can a community be something other than a unit of exclusion? Something which asserts its desires where they are not met with easy compliance, and aggresses against the opposition, and also defends violently when it is aggressed upon? The city around us was throbbing and bleeding out of cracks of compounded touch and rejected touch. It was oozing violent need.

Elaina shook her head. She chuckled her dark little laugh.

But I was taking myself seriously.

I sometimes had the ability of confidence in those days and I was so saddened by the scene before us. I believed she had some greater comprehension, and that her optimism could then be justified. Something learned and real.

I think on the way the followers would prostrate themselves before her, full of inquiries into the nature of the cosmos.

I was the first disciple.

I would kneel like a child and ask for answers.

I begged Elaina, What does it all mean? Who are we protecting ourselves from? Why are we deserving of protection?

Elaina kissed the tip of my nose, her breath smelling of vodka and apricots and old spit. The bile of her stomach. Elaina never breathed upon me rot, as if she were truly made pure by the eternals and not starvation. Even knowing her mortal flesh as I did, my eyes fluttered.

Elaina told me if I was not so beautiful she would not tolerate my simpleness. She tapped the side of my skull, *What is happening in there?*

I imagined I knew some of what was happening in Elaina. I studied her to the point of consumption. Her mannerisms and habits and opinions. Her history. Her reactions and the flavor of her skin.

If I myself was a unit, a solitary one without pawns for protection and battering rams, perhaps I could instead of adjoining myself to others, creating the problem I'd just tried to have Elaina resolve, become others. Become this one other. Become like Elaina's limb or extra mouth. Aaron to Moses. Not entirely alone. Never alone. And if Elaina understood why some people were superior to others, why loving and choosing someone made protecting them, against others, at all cost, "just," then absorbed by her I could understand too. And I could *believe.* I wanted so much to believe there was meaning after all. And so I crawled inside of my obsession. My deification. Even before things had gone so far.

These sorts of conversations came up often among the followers. How to construct a meaningful and egalitarian community. How to be just with one another, despite our biases—our sordid lived lives which tainted even our most pure intentions.

The followers were marxists, anarchists—one a roundly mocked democratic socialist. They saw in Elaina not only the opportunity for a communion with the divine, but in the construction of the compound, an opportunity to recalibrate the most corrupt bits of the society they so abhorred.

Elaina's second husband had been a revered New York congressman who was assassinated before his fiftieth birthday. She had been a shadowy but bitingly sharp leftist presence since the death. Radical. But also, woo woo. Brilliantly insightful, but sometimes, out of touch. She walked a fine line between the spiritual and the secular, and among a growing number of discontents, developed a following.

First in the brownstone, then in Twitter threads, and later around the hearth in the center of the compound, one could hear heartbreakingly earnest conversations. "Where is this world going." Conversations about cryptocurrency investment and internet pornography and reparations. About colonialism, the military budget, the guillotine, radical love and acceptance, martyrdom. How to become more involved in local politics of the region. How to barricade oneself from it all. And Elaina's followers would take themselves so, so seriously. And when in conversing they reached a point of shame at their own ardent aspirations, they would look to Elaina to impart her earned wisdom.

But, so often Elaina would reign over these discussions without ever interfering. It seemed a benevolence to the followers, humility, or an interest in true democracy—but I think she knew her withholding incited their adoration.

The artifice of a community built on faith galled me. The only order came from individuals willing to hog-tie their own realities. If all the disciples had been motivated, like Jesse and I, by love, the overwhelming base urges of the here and now, that I could have at least understood.

But, what kind of society can be built on the now?

7 A.M.

Jesse was trapped. He was trying to convince Elaina
that a tree made a sound in a wood, even if no one was
there to hear it.

Jesse had willfully forgotten that while there might
be dissent allowed among the ranks, only Elaina could
bear the truth, and that any interpretation of reality
that directly disagreed with hers was a threat to the
safety she'd built for us.

There must have been darkness that summer on the
compound, but it seemed to so many of us as if the sun
was always high. It seemed to me that the days always
stretched so joyously long, and that maybe they always
would. That night we could hear music, acoustic guitar
and hand drums. There was an animal being slaugh-
tered for meat, and under a lone tree in an adjacent
field, two men held hands and whispered through their
psychedelics. Lovemaking was still plentiful and public

and I, mostly sober and celibate, had just been allowed to let my cheek linger on the large exposed breast of one of Martha's helpers in the kitchen.

Elaina was at the height of her divinity and it was impossible to imagine her as anything resembling the solitary ember she'd seemed when we left the city. She was ablaze; we were all kindling. Combined our zealotry was a catching beacon, a heat detectable from space.

Elaina was pacing around Jesse as he stammered in his tell-tale way, a stopping voice that suited his gait, and lovemaking, and essence.

Jesse, "Sound waves—"

Jesse, "Consciousness—"

Elaina was traveling on her concave frame around and around the circular table, the heart of the compound's octagonal centerpiece, our little cabin, and she was cackling. Running her small hands around the short hairs on her scalp as though she was trying to comprehend. "Consciousness, you say? Oh, yes of course. God did not give us the gift of full sentience. The path to community which, by His hand, I've labored over and designed to support and protect, to help and lead the solitary into the fold through atonement. No point. An individual could exist on his own and be complete and the nothingness surrounding him would be sufficient and his loneliness would not make him suffer, his mortal shell would not be wasted. Reality is not made by Him but instead what matters is the nothing that came before. What matters is nothing?! Jesse, how can you be part of us when you do not believe in us! You believe in nothing."

Elaina often talked in circles like this, her tail diving into her mouth, manipulating fact to better suit the form she would like to take in a moment.

Jesse, "Reality exists on its own—"

Elaina, "Because it was crafted? Reality is a narrative and God's prophets are his mouthpiece for the pieces of the story he cares to share with us. And if God does not choose to share a part of the story with us, then it does and should not exist to us."

Jesse, "There is nothing—" "But God shares the woods he shares—" "Wouldn't you like to understand?"

Elaina said, "What do I not understand, Jesse?"

Something in Jesse's silence suggested a blasphemy. In the quiet I saw Elaina's face the first time Jesse had penetrated her from behind, curling his right hand around the front of her throat in a way no other man had dared in years. The shocked breath as he pushed her shoulders down below her hips. Her nostrils flared with indignation and delight.

It was only the three of us that night, the night around the round table. Soft lights in windows, in doorways. But no hands gripping the wooden walls or feet other than our own on the floors covered in furs and rugs. If there had been followers milling about the rooms Jesse would never have questioned Elaina in this way. In fact, Jesse and I almost never spoke to Elaina in public, and these nights of our small family unit were growing more and more infrequent as Elaina's interests became wider. As her needs became things we two could not offer her alone. As Jesse became bitter. And, as Elaina's son Immanuel grew older. As his own flock of worshippers flourished, and demanded attention and tending.

Elaina, "If I am Anyone to you, then as Anyone I can only hold so much space for these abstracts. Anyone has duties. Wants. Wants elsewhere." At this Jesse set his palms along his thighs. He closed one of his fists. Once. I saw Elaina notice and smile, and I flushed from my hairline to my collarbone, thinking of the fingers that now gripped the knees, slippery with her. Even after everything, these waves of jealousy would overtake me.

Elaina lowered her voice and, still standing, the white dress she'd taken to wearing around the compound fluttering around her sharp body, leaned forward. "A sound, Jesse? You're talking about divination through isolation. You're talking about monasticism—" Taking his chin in her small palm. "Why not just pursue nirvana without us then?"

I watched them like this, Jesse too angry to pretend to follow her nonsense. Too large for the table.

You could not help but think of Sampson or David as he succumbed to her probe, a slight smile on her face. But Jesse was desperate this night to maintain

some kind of agency. Maybe he saw how little of
himself there was left to lose. How close he was to
being like me. Maybe Jesse remembered his wife, for
who he had been enough, and it gave him courage.

Jesse, "If a man has a vision and no one is there to
see it…?"

Elaina pulled back.

I inserted myself with a warning, Jesse stop.

Elaina laughed. "Oh baby." She stood behind me
and used me as a shield against Jesse's words, hands
on my shoulders. The smells of our old erotics had
been replaced by the scent of desitin, sour breast milk,
bleach, fresh blood from the kitchens.

Elaina, her lisp leaking through, "Baby. He knows it
was not just me. He is teasing."

Jesse, angry now, "Shouldn't YOU be the one
who—"

Jesse, "There has to be—"

Jesse looked through me to Elaina as he spoke. Jesse
was never threatened by me the way I was by him. In
fact, it took him a long time to even notice me, even as
I ate at his table. Even as I sat in chairs and observed
his lovemaking. Even as I trailed him across fields and
rooms. It took him longer still to appreciate my role
in Elaina's world. I do not think Jesse had much imag-
ination—this debate showed a rare spark—and he
certainly could not believe in a dynamic between two
women that might exist at the same ferocity or tenor
as one where a man was present. But neither Jesse or I

were kept by Elaina for our minds.

Elaina gripped at me as if she could draw the energy from my body to convert this nonbeliever. I gave all to her.

Elaina, stepping in front of me, "Hush."

It seemed not only Jesse, but some of the followers who had begun to congregate around the cherrywood table, staggering as if through the sleepy haze of their pleasure, and also the stars which hung low in the wide Idaho sky—still gray and blue with the last of the sun—were waiting for her next words. Elaina relished in this attention and pulled from my body my aware-ness of it.

Elaina, "God has made himself known to me."

And all took in a heavy breath with the truth of it.

I met Elaina when I was nineteen. I recognized her at a party my fiancé had brought me to, sitting on a long white couch and drinking gin. She was aging, but I remembered her twiggy physique and platinum blonde hair. She had always stood out to me in her small roles in films from the nineties. Mostly mistresses and party girls, before she met her second husband. The night I met Elaina her face was puffy from drugs and drinking, and she had already begun cropping her hair close to her scalp. Her body though, was still rail thin and expressive. Her laugh was still deep and compelling. She was sitting in the corner surrounded by a group of men. Each was attending to her, bringing her food

and drink, smiling at the smallest thing she said—
even while younger and more agreeable female party
members hovered behind them.

My fiancé at the time was a photographer I'd met
on a shoot. Tall, older than me, but not too much.
Ineloquent. I thought it was the most one could hope
for in this life. Insurance. Commitment. Admiration as
object, even. The way he'd moved me on our first shoot
like a marionette, the way I'd responded when moved.
To me, this seemed enough.

But, I had not yet met Elaina.

I believe Elaina played this trick on many of us. We
were content, even happy, and then we knew better. As
if her own dissatisfaction were catching. Her gift was
to see your powerlessness. She gave you liberation, to
quickly strip it away.

When Elaina first spoke to me it was to ask me
about my ring, a lapis lazuli stone embedded in old
silver. I told her it was an antique. I told her my fiancé
knew how much I loved the ocean.

Elaina, "So your fiancé has committed a violence?
He has taken this thing you love from you? Made you
believe he is part of that love, even the thing you love
itself?"

Elaina, without asking, took my hand in hers.
Smiling to herself, she twisted the ring off my finger.
The band usually stuck around my knuckle, but when
Elaina pulled, my body seemed to shift in size to allow
her whatever she wanted with it. The ring, so easily sep-

arated from me, looked cheap in the fluorescent light of the host's living room. "What a cruel trick." Looking in my boyfriend's direction, she laughed. "What a bastard."

Elaina, my ring in her left hand, placed her right on my elbow—a finger stroked the protruding bone like a beckon—and I knew then that before this moment I'd known nothing of desire, or power, or touch.

It is funny to me now, because Elaina is like the ocean. She is too slippery to hold and forever threatening to overtake you. Truly, between the two, Elaina is perhaps more like our understanding of the sea than the waves themselves. That she was always the trap laid for me.

I do not think I ever put the ring back on my finger after she graced me with a knowledge of her. This forbidden fruit.

My fiancé was baleful and desperate when I returned it to him. He pinned me over and over against the white drywall of his apartment. You can't do this. You're not someone who can make it on your own. The sweat on the fat of his palms disgusted me. The water and meat beneath the callouses.

But, he was right. Autonomy was truly not the gift Elaina gave me. Only awareness of what I would be leaving the garden for.

When I offered myself to Elaina, she set me nude in front of a window for any passerby to see, and as I wept ran just the bone of her wrist along the cords of my neck until I came.

The night Jesse and Elaina sat bickering at the table was so many years later. That girl shuddering in the window, flushed red down her neck and chest, removed and strange from the one who now whispered around the hearth. Each concession to Elaina's love had been, what may appear to an outsider, to be a dwindling of my person. But really, each concession was also a portal through which I could climb to new heights of devotion. Each night tending to her tired body. Or her child, Immanuel, wishing he was ours alone. The change in my mind after caretaking, a new crack of consciousness. The only thing that had not transformed since that first party was Elaina's security in my absolute subservience.

That night at the table, Jesse, for the first time, looked at me. Needed me.

Jesse, "She wants me to give up too much."

I did not know what he wanted, permission to remain apart, or a reason to surrender. I spoke not to him, but instead turned my face up towards Elaina's and whispered, If you have complete faith, you are willing to make complete sacrifice. Offer complete subjugation.

I licked oil from the morning's breakfast off my lips in anticipation of her praise, but Elaina smiled not down at me, but across the table at her prodigal paramour.

Martha entered the room at the end of the conversation and knelt a little by Elaina's elbow. Elaina in her sheer dress and barefoot, but with that low hum of power still swirling around her and in which we were all caught.

Martha moved with a hurried dignity. She could not be shocked or surprised, only disappointed. The space between her breasts and her neck was long and bore a series of skin discolorations that looked like a fern. Other than me Martha was the first of the followers. Other than Jesse she was the boldest. Unmotivated by desire, Martha was also the most devout of us all.

Martha did not need to say Immanuel's name but only raise her eyebrows slightly and Elaina followed Martha from the room.

Jesse and I sat alone as the followers dissipated around us, returning to their earlier activities.

After our abandonment—sometimes I want to ask Jesse to pinch me so he can tell me he has heard me, that I am real. But then I would have to trust that Jesse too exists, like the sound, without Elaina's acknowledgment of him. It is a final betrayal I cannot manage.

To be together and still be so unobserved and terrible.

Jesse admitted to me at the table that day, when Elaina could not hear him, that perhaps he was wrong. Maybe it was ego. I wanted that night to tell Jesse I would teach him how to better submit, but even that seemed hubris.

So, instead we two just sat there, for many hours. Waiting for Elaina to return.

8 A.M.

The motel has a few free snacks. Microwavable
popcorn. Tea. Tastykakes. The granola bars are the
same ones they used to serve for breakfasts in grade
school. It is a wonder to me that I am the same person
as the one who would unwrap them in the gymnasium
before morning classes. That my daughter might one
day curl her hair around her fingers and wrists in a
lunch hall. I think, she is part me, and it does not seem
so bad.

I have always liked repetition and sameness.
Objects, textures, behaviors. Afraid of what might fall
apart with even the slightest aberration. And we have
been in such a state of movement, it seems since I left
New York with Elaina my only certainty was her.

As a child I was so rigid as to refuse to eat off
anything but a small set of peach ceramic dishes my
parents had received for their wedding. It was my

mother's favorite color. Too pale to be a flower, just red enough to resemble dry earth.

One night my sister and I held each other through a particularly violent fight in the kitchen, the thudding of bodies and a full throated howling from our mother. The sound of a shatter, and another, and another. Shrieks.

We woke to a kitchen full of shards and a front door left ajar. I put my sister in her pink raincoat and galoshes and packed her bag with her school books and pencils, and we tiptoed over the full set of destroyed pink dishware. We held hands on our way to school through a deep low fog that covered the earth and made it impossible to see more than three feet ahead. When we arrived at the school we were given granola bars, these same ones they have in the hotel, in all-white plastic packaging. Chocolate milk. My sister held my waist as she chewed.

I think despite myself of Immanuel.

A spirit tells me it is dangerous to go there, to think of what might have been. The spirit says they withered in their life, waiting to return to people who no longer existed. We all change so quickly. Are you the same woman you were at that first party? I say already this morning I have said I am, all the way back. And besides, I don't like the ship game. Elaina would make me play it too often and the answer I gave was never right.

I begin making coffee with a waxy paper cup and water from the bathroom.

Jesse looks at me from the bed. His voice and eyes are still feminized by the dream, but he is returning. Jesse pulls his legs off the bed. He sighs, a weight over him. He asks if there's anything I need.

I tell him no. We have coffee. We have some food, and I push a granola bar that I have unwrapped for myself into his hands. Jesse rises, slow, walks to the bathroom to piss with the granola bar still in his hand. The thick odor and comforting steady stream that means he is in working order. The clatter of the porcelain as the seat falls.

When Jesse leaves the bathroom, he begins dressing as he eats, pulling on his boots while little crumbs fall around the room.

I ask, Where are you going?

Jesse, "I just—"

Jesse, "I just need a little air."

A spirit, He is not coming back.

Jesse does not look at me as he walks to the door, closes it behind him. I am frightened by the sudden cold air that follows, the lavender light that means the sun is finally rising behind the stormy clouds.

The spirits are noisy, excited by the sudden taste of the outside. But the one who gave me warning is somber.

This all began, like these things do, after a long period of stagnation. Elaina's love for me then was too thin to catch a breath inside of.

I had been squatting in Elaina's brownstone for five years by then. Elaina cooked. I cleaned. We lived off of her royalties from her days as a young starlet and mysterious cash donations from admirers and court ordered checks from ex husbands. Elaina didn't like to leave the house and she didn't like me taking jobs. Upon acquiring me she was determined to keep me to herself—though when we'd first met she'd hung a long string of my test shots along a clothesline in the hallway. Would parade guests past them. My unarranged limbs and my eyes like a gazelle's. My adolescent nipples in a smile. As a unit, Elaina and I became impenetrable, keeping house all day while Elaina said her prayers, corresponded with her new devotees, attended her social clubs.

With little to do, I'd taken up the hobby of listening to Elaina's neighbors argue. You could hear them through the kitchen walls. The woman weeping.

"Stop apologizing." You could rarely make out the words of the woman, but you could always hear this from the husband. There was no point to her apologizing, he would say. None. And, Stop. The volume would rise and fall, and rise again.

Elaina would listen too. And we would look at each other; at least we are not like that. But also sometimes Elaina would frown and slip her hands down the front of me, clinging and rocking from behind the way she would when she wanted.

There is always a day in early summer when the heat

becomes too intense to feel uncomplicated pleasure in, and on this day the couple again began fighting. Louder. More. They were too intense too quick and just a few feet beyond the drywall. Then suddenly, so soft. I could feel the sweat between my breaths in tremors as the husband said, "Do you think God has forgiven you?" The husband again, "Then why should I?" The wife's weeping audible.

I was clattering around the kitchen doing dishes. The husband sounded tired, and were I not so used to the argument I barely would have been able to make him out. I paused my hands, turned off the faucet to offer my full attention.

"Please."

The husband, "Please, stop apologizing." And, "I cannot forgive you."

Sobs.

And we heard the front door open, and close.

Elaina was in the kitchen with me. She moved herself around my body to sit on the counter, resting her forearms on her spread knees, and for several moments we listened to the weeping with reverence. Until it stopped.

Elaina turned to me then and, in this sudden and oppressive quiet, asked if I thought God had forgiven her. I did not used to believe in those sorts of things, but telling Elaina this never did anything but upset her. And Elaina so infrequently asked my thoughts or advice, so I was honored to feel so close to her inner

life. So, instead of responding, I was quiet. Let it be.
I asked Elaina, What might God be upset with you
about? I asked Elaina, What have you done that is so
wrong?

Elaina said, "I might not have done it yet."

The husband never returned, but I saw the wife on
her back patio often, chain smoking and haggard—
picking at her face with long jagged nails.

Elaina, watching from behind me, told me she was
tired of the city.

Elaina, "I want to go home."

We planned what was sold to me as a two-month
trip out West. I imagined we'd rent out the house, buy
a used car, luxuriate on long stretches of highway. Stop
wherever we might feel compelled to. But always, I was
sure we'd come back.

I asked Elaina, is there some coordinate where we
should arrive? Will there be family to visit? Friends to
see? Elaina would shake her head dismissively, like the
questions themselves were ridiculous.

In the car Elaina was often sick. The motion of the
road nauseated her. The scenery was smattered with
blood stains from genocide and she heard little girls
crying in every ramshackle home we passed. I would
try to comfort her. I would try to tell her stories but she
could not tolerate my voice by then. She did not want
to hear sounds from me, but instead immerse herself in
the suffering.

The door is closed behind Jesse, and he has not returned.

I turn on the television to drown out the memories and the spirits who are convinced I will be alone here forever. The additional voices at least create a noxious rotation of non-language sounds the spirits cannot break through. I look to my stomach. Hello Baby, it is just us now. But there is no responding surge. I sigh. I imagine my daughter years from now restricting access to a clubhouse or bedroom. With a blanket over her head so she can be alone. These images are comforting to me. Maybe that is just the way she is, secretive. I can love someone with a need for privacy. I can handle that.

An episode of the previous night's *Bachelorette* plays while I fold pants and towels and turn the water on for a shower, allowing the steam to fill the cold room.

Between modeling jobs in New York, hotels and ready rooms, I would watch *The Bachelor* with mobs of starving girls. We were all such funny little puritans to be symbols of sex. One of my first friends when I was fifteen would become so flustered being touched by stylists in the nude, she would cross herself. We would watch the television contestants gossip and backstab and she was incredulous. Women would not be so cruel to each other. And I would kiss her.

I always thought *The Bachelor* made sense, though. A nation of women vying, cutthroat, for the love of a man. This I have never doubted the veracity of. But I have a hard time believing in the reverse. The stakes seem too low. Wasn't Helen even, in the end, a scapegoat? A thing to be replaced?

Elaina would accuse me of misogyny were she here, rather than congratulate me for my thinking, and also would gesture towards her own form as the exception to the rule that a woman could not be an individual of worth.

A centipede on the white wall.

A stinkbug trapped under a lampshade sizzles over and over again against a bulb.

I am growing used to the hum of the television and cannot fully drown out the spirit's soft voices. Elaina used to translate them for me.

Elaina, *What are the angels telling you now, baby? Who do they want you to see?*

A spirit, prompted, would then speak repetitively. The Star is a tarot card. In readings, the Star is the opposite of the Devil who strips us of our faith in the future. I would tell Elaina today there is a mother convincing her daughter it will be over before she knows it. There is a man cutting himself with a dull knife, serrated, and he runs it back and forth over his inner forearm. There is a writer who is refusing to take off their shoes because the soles of their feet are black with filth and sores.

I imagine Elaina listening, the way she would during the time when she said she loved me. Her head tilted slightly to one side. The slight smile like she was discovering something in me.

I turn the volume on the television up.

I step into the shower. The more I think on it, the more my thoughts on *The Bachelor* feel true—it feels violent and cruel to pretend they aren't. Twelve women vying over one man is not the same as the reverse. But I should change this belief before the baby is born. I should save her from these projections and look only with optimism.

I am always hoping to bore the spirits with my thoughts, which I think they can read.

They should have grown tired of me by now, self-absorbed and small. They should long for their primary host, if that is in fact what Elaina was. I wonder what the spirits think of my naked body, bloated and heavy. Do they notice me at all or are they so consumed with a desire to be noticed there is no space for them to do the same? I understand this state.

I look at myself, showing now, but softly. A thickness. I long for a moment to be the shape I was when I was wanted. I long to offer this shape to Jesse, if only for a little more safety. But, then I apologize to my daughter. I say, I am happy you are here with me.

My hair is dry. It has been. The Western air. The motel shampoo. Stepping into the water I hold the warmth for a bit. Force extra conditioner through the tangles with my fingers, move some of the runoff over the stretch marks on my upper thighs and stomach and breasts.

I shot up as a child. Five-eleven—and I have been

this tall since I was twelve. I was thin when I was young, half hunger half growing too fast. Now I place my hands on my stomach and try to be kind, for the girl's sake again. I think, maybe she will be beautiful, but not so much that it will be a problem. Maybe she will be smarter than me, or very talented in mathematics. But again, not so much that it draws unwanted attention. I think, maybe she will be competent and happy. Maybe I will teach her to see the world as glorious as Elaina believed it to be, and if she perceives it as such, maybe it will be that way.

I thumb again between my fingers the coarse and broken ends of my hair.

The storm has started up again, but I think not for long. A growl of thunder muffles the individual interviews, the playback of the episode's drama. This region of Montana was shared by six, or maybe seven, tribes for hunting. The river drew buffalo and belonged to no one. I think I should not bring another child to this land where we have sinned so much, but, I do not know where else to take her.

I think about Jesse. I think of his body inside of the storm. Is he still cold from the dream? I feel a pinch in my chest at that, his woman's body, lost in the snow and tripping over her petticoats. I place my right hand against my lower back and close my eyes while pain moves through me. Half a heaviness, half a want. My legs opening to memory of wanting fingers, the steam cradling me with phantom hands. A million silent hands.

Condensation runs along the glass and white tile. I sense how sequestered I am from the earth and sky in the small dingy room. But there is water. A spirit cups her hands beneath her chin to catch her own tears, but she is laughing. The Devil's power rests in the illusion that nothing else exists. The same spirit is jerking off again, half clothed, back to me.

I hear Elaina's voice in my head when I shiver at the thunder. Elaina never took these storms seriously. A memory of her barefoot on the compound. Perching herself on the roof and looking into the sky. I think maybe one day Elaina and Immanuel will recede in my consciousness. That eventually every aspect of living will not make me think of them. But I also cannot imagine that this could be true.

I can hear on the television the sound of a fight between the men on the show. Low voices rising in octaves and the occasional laugh which is an invitation, "You wanna fight me?"

The storm is furious like it knows it is about to pass. Sheets of horizontal rain but already you can see blue light behind the clouds.

The final suds from my hair and body rinsing down my calves and feet. And as I watch them circle the drain, I see I have begun to bleed.

9 A.M.

I'm sorry. I know people only like to hear the dreams of
the people they love. But I had a dream last night too.
In my dream I saw a blackbird and the span of its wings
transformed suddenly into Jesse's long body which I
held as I slept so tight I collapsed atom by atom into his
flesh. I could also see in this dream Jesse's body curled
around Elaina's as she labored, her back leaning against
his chest, his hands on her belly, hers pressing against
his knees—even as the tops of my feet were tickled
by the hair on his calves. I moved my fingers to search
for open air, but in the dream I found Elaina as she
groaned, as the head began to crown.

I saw a flower. The flower's skirt appeared both
as petals, purple and deep blue veins, and as Elaina's
fingers interlaced with Jesse's. The knuckles and bones
making a checkered pattern under the long toes of an
infant cased in blood and membrane. The dream then
became memory. The bow of Jesse's body as he was

introduced to Immanuel.

In my dream I heard the first rain of this morning's incoming storm, and the soft splash of each water droplet colliding with the asphalt of the parking lot was the sound of Jesse's voice—which had told me so sweetly just the night before that he had chosen me, that I was safe and the home we would build would not be rivaled in joy or security—whispering in Elaina's ear how he had never been and would never again be so happy, so engorged, so in love.

In my dream an audible hiss of a flash of the lightning leaving a cloud became the sound of Elaina smiling. The rare stretch of skin in her cheek like an old rubber band.

Jesse, "What if another life isn't—" "Living—"

Jesse, "You're glad you're alive?"

Jesse, our holy spirit to my Joseph.

We had spent the day with Immanuel. I taught him a new song which I would sing, and he would copy. I taught him. Yo ho ho, half steps down. *Yo ho ho*, the god child echoed. And again, and again, until he learned the first verse. Then I began to pester him with alliteration and scales. He giggled and breathed heavy, trying to keep up. Then I tricked him—the notes rolled up so high he could not follow anymore but only instead scream. I picked him up high into the air and he let the call ring out. His voice was sweet and strong. The sweetness Jesse's, the strength Elaina's. A buck and three deer turned their heads in our direction. I was laughing, and Immanuel pulled at my arms for the ground and in the grass also began to laugh. A final bit of mimicry.

I was the servant who had rushed turkey baster after turkey baster of sperm into the rooms of our cabin's most holy lady.

Elaina had wanted the conception to be, "Immaculate." "Pure."

I was afraid of the result of such an experiment, but when Immanuel was born I marveled at him, even knowing all I did. I was in awe at the true divinity of the collaboration.

Pick a pack of peppers, I would sing. And Immanuel would repeat. And although I hate the spirits now, I would have enjoyed their more animated presence then, to have someone else to witness the tender euphoria. Perhaps later to have someone brush aside my own howl of untranslatable feeling to the woods. The spirits would tell me my state was nothing. One of many states of pain shared by many others.

Often Jesse and I were charged with Immanuel's care while Elaina tended to the flock and Martha the kitchens, so we were allowed to run in circles in green fields lined in small white flowers. Sweet peas, cotton bushes, yellow butterflies would find themselves in a circlet, crowning his head. Then seeing our delight at his beauty, Immanuel would sprint. And he was his mother's son, running farther, just too far to see.

But, even as Jesse and I leaned against one another in the grass—*Will you go for him? Should I?*—always he returned. And I would call his name and I would scoop him into my arms. Yo ho ho. Jesse would kiss the top of both our heads.

But this last day, I could not feel the same pleasure at the light. Immanuel's presence instead caused me pain. I turned to Jesse whose eyes were closed too, avoiding some bright magnesian flare.

I discovered the pregnancy only two days before this conversation, pissing on a stick in a grocery store stall, tucked between frozen meats and ice cream and preserved dinners ready to activate. Away from the compound. Martha had been lurking around my shoulder too often lately, as if there was a scent to me.

One dark night the autumn before, I'd found Elaina not at the foot of Immanuel's toddler bed, as she promised she would be, nor in her prayer room, nor in the kitchens, but instead on the roof. She was swaying, her toes slipping on the tiles, her shaved head reflecting the moon's blue glow. She tried to push me away as I approached.

I told Elaina it was too dark for god to see her, us, anyone. Wasn't she the one who taught me that Akhenaten himself was her lineage, and as the sun rotated away so did god from his children. To have some rest from our misery?

I told her Immanuel was crying. He was. A pain of a

sound that snuck up so as to be visible between us. But it seemed Elaina had grown bored with the baby.

Me too. Elaina no longer wanted me in her rooms. She no longer wanted to teach me lessons, or to seek quiet secret validations. Instead she would spread her palms amongst the followers, stroking back the sweat of their brow, preaching her gospels. She would rend her garments in the open air to mourn the end of every day. And she could not see me. Her body so altered I could only remember the touch of her finger on the tip of my nose, the bone beneath my breast. But the memory was removed from the thing before me. Only a shudder. A suffering in my gut.

And that night, or some other night like it, I arrived at Jesse's door. He might have looked at me disappointed, and led me in, and called me Elaina's name while inside me. I might have snuck out before the sun could spy on us together. Or, he might have looked for me himself.

I don't know what I thought would happen.

After the pregnancy test I met Jesse again in the parking lot, his long legs straddling two parallel yellow lines, and I placed my fourth finger between my two front teeth. And he opened the passenger side door.

We stayed up the whole night sitting on a concrete tire stop in a Taco Bell parking lot, smoking Parliaments and eating. I told him I was craving the most mortal of things, in order to know what we had been

missing. My mouth sticky with ash and nacho cheese, I
did not even have the courage to ask him.

Sometimes when the followers arrived at the
compound they would kneel in the dirt, kiss it with
their foreheads. Then they would turn to Elaina, the
wife of the sun and the mother of their savior.
     They would kiss the feet of god's son with their
tears.
     Immanuel would stand very still, and if he tried
to run, or if he would squirm beneath Elaina's hands,
Jesse would put his fingers to his lips from among the
throngs of believers and shake his head. And Immanuel
would smile.
     I asked Jesse, Could we make a God too?
     Jesse shook his head.
     I asked Jesse again, Could I make a God?
     I did not say it would be as perfect as Immanuel.

We returned to the compound when the sun was rising.
We smelled of grease and smoke and it intensified the
hot colors of the approaching orb. Elaina walked across
the field behind the yard, her white dress reflecting
prisms of light and throwing it against the grass.
     I lost all the breath in my body with grief. With
want. With wrath.

I step out of the shower. I wrap my hair in one towel,
my body in another. I think I might need both towels

and remove the one from my hair, then I think the towels are white, who will get my stains out? Elaina would always tip cash for the staff wherever we stayed; she liked to signal her virtues. I would remember to get cash. I would remember to tip. I would minimize the damage I inflict always with my existence.

I dry myself, blotting at the thin red blood between my legs. Put on my panties, roll toilet paper in a tight wad and place it between my cotton underwear and the skin of my lips and upper thighs.

I look in the mirror. I think, maybe the stress of the past few days, maybe it will all go away now. I do not think of the small bag I've packed full of Martha's children's old baby clothes.

I move over this. I do not think where I will go.

The spirits are whispering in a frenzy. I do not need their judgments.

I walk past the woman catching her tears and the man jerking off and think, A drink then.

The closest bar is an hour walk but I think it will be worth it. My body aches but the movement will be a respite from the mind.

I look at the open door to the bathroom and imagine a maid or Jesse discovering it as it is now.

I lean in the doorway. I kneel on the floor and press my palms against the cool tile. Then I run my right fingers through the red blood and watch the long sashes of it as I lead the strands to the drain.

It is sometimes so hard to remember I am a body.

That all I am made up of is these cells and if you puncture me I will leak away into nothing. And then sometimes it is so easy. Watching the water turn pink, then a little yellow, then clear.

When I would talk to Elaina like this, she would tell me how annoying I was to suddenly discover the ephemeral nature of existence. *Ah, baby girl, the first among us to discover death.*

The storm is long passed by the time I've gotten on my boots and pulled my hair back. Folding the strands over one another feels familiar too, and grounding. Left, right, left, right, as the TV continues to play. A rat scratches from inside the nightstand. A spirit is rehearsing how she will lie about the abortion to her husband, another is singing a lullaby. I leave the television on to keep the spirits company. The rat bolts towards the bathroom. I see it approach the clean mound of flesh in the corner. I sever the rat's way with my hand. I pull the mass to my heart.

The toilet paper in my panties is already full by the time I am ready to leave, so I fold up one of the pure white washcloths on the sink's counter. You can see the bulge if you look closely. But I tie it in place with dental floss and can walk without it shifting. I've packed a second in my coat pocket, just in case.

I line the ice bucket and place what I've found in the shower inside. I secure the lid. I close my eyes, just a little, imagining.

My breasts are heavy and I want to linger.

Maybe I keep the television on to keep the ice bucket company as well?

I pull on my boots and Jesse's thick coat and close the door behind me.

The winter light is too strong.

I travel a little ways, turn back to check the door is locked, travel, turn back to check again. Like I am trying to keep something safe. I see a man peering out of the center room which houses a reception desk. He is wearing a baseball cap and his arms are thick with black and red tattoos. I place the motel key in my bra and feel the plastic card seal to the cold sweat on my breast. Moisture from the morning's storm which is still in the air. I gesture like I am taking a shot to the man in the hotel. Point in either direction. He gives me a thumbs up and points me to the right, down a highway that leads into town. I check once more that the door is locked, as though there is something worth protecting inside, and then I begin to walk.

Long meadows of dead grass and cattle surround the black tar of the road and you can see the mountains behind them, peaked with snow although we have none in the valley. A car pulls to the shoulder and the passenger rolls down his window, offers me a ride. A second car does this. Men. I say no thank you sirs and smile very sweet.

I am used to this kind of traveling. Often during one of Elaina's moods she would pull over, open the door, tell me if I was so intent on upsetting her while she was driving, wasn't it best if I just walk? Always on the topic of theology. The afterlife. Whether we were already living in hell, or whether we were destined for it. The baby who just discovered death has been blessed with a premier comprehension of the soul which she developed over a period of five whole minutes.

It was the one thing she could not get me to stop saying. I would insist that the way I believe in a soul is only that I believe in love. I believe that the pull I feel towards Elaina, or Jesse, my sister, the boy god Immanuel, is an energy that cannot be just of one time.

Elaina would say, Appropriation.

Connecting with old truth, I said. It wouldn't be truth if it was only mine.

And that is how I became so accustomed to walking on the side of highways. I can mostly recommend it, but there is, if you are not drinking, too much time to think.

I remember now how my dream ended.

In the dream Jesse turned to me, holding Immanuel and nodding towards Elaina, asleep after the labor. Jesse asked me, gesturing towards our sleeping prophet, "Isn't she the most beautiful?"

Jesse said, "Look she's—"

Stopped.

Jesse, "She's made a soul."

10 A.M.

The months after my father left my mother, my mother
was so forlorn she would not leave her back room. She
would not bathe and seemed barely to eat. My sister
and I could hear her weeping through the door, at
which she would throw accusations he could not hear
and sometimes moan some long and airy thing.

It was soon summer and without the school's provi-
sions, we would grow hungry after long days away from
my mother's pain. At first I would make ramen. I would
watch an infant in the neighborhood for an evening
or two, exchange a ten dollar bill for a case of twenty,
place the square noodles in the pot. My sister always
wanted more though, and often I would not give it to
her, preferring to be full myself. The rush of shame here
is similar to the pulsing blood in your limbs and head
when you had completed everything there was to find.
After binging I felt warm and satisfied, as if I had been
exposed to human touch.

I would buy cans of cold soup from the dollar store
and Texas Toast which we dipped in watery food bank
ketchup. Handfuls of brown sugar. Bags of marshmal-
lows and generic corn flakes. I loved the sugar water
in a can of sweet peas. We would bring the food to our
room and listen to our mother's moans—she was too
exhausted to wail—and feast.

In the visions Elaina began to have before we left, she
said she saw flocks. Hordes. Masses of followers whom
she could offer the light to.

I would ask, How would she feed them? Who
tended to them? Would they arrange themselves in
gendered bunks or nuclear family structures? Would
there be a nursery? Would there be scriptures? Would
there be crops?

Elaina said only, *Have faith.*

Elaina met the first believer, beyond her small circle
of desperate socialites and rejected artists in the city,
outside of the YMCA in Spokane. We were in the city
collecting frivolous goods we had left behind in New
York, Elaina's favorite espresso beans and scented soaps.
I was hoping to spend an evening eating good food I
had not cooked myself, or lounging in a local park.

Martha was sitting outside the center with her three
sons, waiting for the center to open. Her youngest was
six months and tugging at her collar like he was hungry.
They were all four in clean T-shirts and basketball shorts,
including Martha herself, her delicate coloring concealed.

Martha caught Elaina's eyes, and it was like love. Elaina closed her eyes, savoring the discovery, then began to walk towards the family. I saw her intention and protested, Please Elaina, they need real help. But Elaina was sure of her gift.

Martha looked up at Elaina. Her lips were turned down on the sides and there were dark shadows created by the intensity of her furrowed brow. She asked what it was we wanted.

Elaina said, "To offer your family salvation."

Martha laughed. She said she'd been acquainted with our lord and savior Jesus Christ and she didn't need to see any more of him. I wavered again pulling at Elaina's hand, Come we're not wanted here.

Elaina ignored me and knelt on the ground before Martha, not on one knee but two. Elaina asked Martha her name, Martha gave it, still scowling. Elaina said, "Help me understand why you are here." I offered to play with the children while they talked.

After several hours of Elaina eliciting from Martha her childhood, her marriage, her sexuality, her passions, even her dreams the night before, the circumstances of a final betrayal which had landed her in a friend's living room alone with three children, Elaina hinted again to Martha a way out. Elaina suggested, with that same effortless wisdom with which she had removed my engagement ring, "What if I truly have seen God?" "What if your struggles are universal, what if together we have gotten off track." And, "I can bring you, finally, home."

It was through Martha's conversion that Elaina became holy.

This is the strategy we would use to acquire the members of Elaina's flock. We would listen, and easily after hearing from their own mouths the horror of their lives in America, they would fold to our truth.

But before the rest, soon after Martha came Georgette, a greasy fry cook so neglected she all but disintegrated into Elaina's upheld palm. For a while it was just us women and Martha's children, nesting in the most central building. Four women, who after our first conversation with Elaina, did not need to say the ways we were alike out loud. Together we no longer felt fragile, nor defeated by life. Under Elaina's tutelage we instead became an eight-armed beast of the sun.

In the months that followed a few men joined, homeless and trying to get clean. I avoided them and kept to childcare, but Martha and Elaina spent most of their days with the new arrivals, sharing our gospel. And then, Elaina wrote home, and all the brainwashed bartenders and smitten suitors from Bushwick arrived with their own money and plans, and they were asked to answer to Martha and Georgette, Elaina's right and left, much as I answered to Elaina. Together we would feast on bourgeois delights while murmuring to one another what a shame the rest of the world should want. While congratulating ourselves on becoming so self-sufficient and enlightened. The family money and the art money and the blood money, all the same, went to the shared pot.

The follower's tables were soon garnished with goat cheese, and venison, and rich chocolate cakes, and wine. Both Elaina and I have a weakness for wine. There seemed always to be more gifts from the followers, but also we learned to milk and slaughter and ferment. We adopted a hive. Elaina would bless what we sowed. Bless us, for sowing. There would be feasts for the phases of the moons and every celebration of a day of birth and the harvest and sometimes only because Elaina was pleased with us. And no one was ever hungry.

To me these feasts seemed not to sate the followers, but instead incite greater and greater desire. The believers would feast to bursting because they desired more of Elaina, more of their god.

I approach the bar up the town's main road and lean myself against the wall. It is cold today and there are few people on the street. I pull Jesse's coat around my face to protect from a biting wind. I can feel that I will need to change the washcloth again. I tell myself it can only be a little blood, that I am imagining things. But the cloth is heavy in my pants. My chest is constricting and I am nauseous. I notice how alone I am without Jesse in this empty town outside of this empty bar. I can see where the town begins and ends and beyond that, mountains, plains, white ice. The big sky that arches eternally. Whose infinity is visceral from my spot against the brick wall. My feet were in pain but now I cannot feel them at all. Besides walking back to the motel, there is nowhere else for miles. Butte is a half an hour drive and more expensive. I count the money in my pocket, fifty dollars. I finger it over and over. One afternoon in the bar will take it all and at least the terror will be softer for it. The voices quieter. When I return to the spirits, they will only be slippery in my periphery, not solid enough to crush me beneath them.

I finger again both the card in my bra and the money in my pocket.

The blood too is a finite concrete thing. The blood is slipping out of me. The blood makes the body real. The body is all I really have. The Elaina in my mind whispers to me, *Baby, you're giving me a headache.*

A woman pulls into the parking lot in a dusty red pickup and walks over to where I am waiting. She looks at me, alone, pale but clean, shivering. Not from around here. The bulge in my pants where cotton capillaries are filling with my blood, my empty but round stomach, are both covered by Jesse's coat. I wave a little and follow her, as a question. The woman considers, then pats my back a few times. Opens the bar's doors, gestures. "Alright then honey. Come on in and have a seat."

The walk along the way has slowed the spasms of my stomach, but after standing still for even these few moments they are back and I hold myself up by pressing against a nearby wall.

I say, Is that a bathroom I can use?

The woman nods, I thank her and tell her I'll be

back soon as she begins to pull chairs off counters and stack them in long rows along the bar.

In the bathroom I find that, yes, the blood has filled the washcloth and is dripping down my thighs again, the inside of my denim wet. I pull the edges of the cloth away to where it has sealed dry against my pubic hair and wipe myself down with warm water, throwing the washcloth in the bottom of the bin beneath the sink, hoping no one will smell it. In the mirror my face seems fleshless, shriveled, my cheeks a puckered texture and the skin around my eyes dark, when just this morning I had told Jesse how full of life I felt. I vomit the granola bar into the sink and wash it down with my hand.

When I leave the bathroom I see there is already another woman at the bar. Slumped. If I look gaunt she looks skeletal, with bleach blonde hair, visibly gray from the roots, and the kind of jacket they wear in factories. Nylon and thick. She has in front of her a tall glass of what could be water, but which I think is probably vodka, and she is sucking it down through a black plastic straw. The end hangs from her mouth and down her lower lip and chin.

I sit two seats away from her.

I wait in the calm dark air of the bar. Warming myself. Only a little light passing through cracks. I have outrun even the spirits. It is so quiet.

In the first months after the birth, Elaina would not be taken from Immanuel's side. Martha and I took care

of the changing and bathing while she rocked herself
near the child, whispering, hands over her chest and
only opening them for feeding, and often resistantly.
Our Mary a ghoul. Despite Elaina's protestations
that I would spoil the child, that he would become
dependent on mortal love, I rocked Immanuel longer
when she was not looking. Hey sweet Manny. Hello my
main man. It was too easy to undermine her during this
period, and so less satisfying.

After the birth, Elaina seemed to spend most of her
time in some other realm. She looked so unlike the dewy
deity I held in my arms, that I thought how much more
like Jesse he seemed to me then, and therefore, myself.
It made me love Elaina freshly too, with deep sympathy.
I felt a soft puffing up with care for her that I had never
known, her new weaknesses exhilarating.

One night, touched as I was, and Elaina seemingly so
deeply and defiantly elsewhere, I told the living god a story,
but I did not at the time know where it had come from.

It is so calm in the bar, I can hear trains nearby. The
wheels rattle on the rails like a storybook. I remember
driving with Immanuel outside the confines of the
compound. The fields were golden and the sun almost
green in the winter light. I remember waiting for the
long cars, counting them as they passed and missing
them when they were gone. I think this bar is where I
came up with the story I told to Immanuel that night.
To keep him closer.

11 A.M.

The woman to my right at the bar seems much shorter
than even five feet, with paper-thin skin and teeth
black from tobacco and meth. I am conscious of the
enormity of my body and flesh in proximity to her. She
wears small scars over her cheeks and neck that remind
me of Jesse, and her wrists are as thin as three of my
fingers. Her eyes are a watery blue, almost transparent.
They reflect light from the town outside.

The bartender has finished unstacking chairs and
shifting objects and is now removing plastic wrap from
bottle tops. Chopping lemons and limes. I can see all
three of us reflected in the mirror. The bartender is
beautiful, although she is also no longer young, with a
full chest, exposed so you can see the soft wrinkles in
the center of the cleavage. Wing-tipped eyeliner. We
might all be the same age, but life shows on us so differ-
ently we could also be three different generations.

I can feel the bartender watching me and the

woman to my right with the peripheral vision of seemingly many eyes, not just two. The sensation reminds me of Elaina, and also my father who would wear sunglasses on the back of his head while taking drunken afternoon naps. The bartender is talking to a man in the kitchen while we remain under observation. The bartender and the man commune in half sentences as he moves out or she moves in. She is angry at him, but in a way that feels to me like desire. I feel I am very good at knowing these things now, it is a gift given through a history of errors.

I am less confident in my assessment of the woman to my right, but maybe that is because she seems more like me than the maybe lovers do with their shoulders pulled back and their confident frustrated tension. The woman to the right might collapse into herself at any moment. I too allow myself to feel the oppressive heaviness of living, pretending I am as beautiful as a diminished star awaiting a final delightful compression, then a sweet warm forever density. A black calm mass.

Since Elaina introduced me to the spirits, bars have become one of the only quiet places for me, where I don't have to hear a teenager in his mother's lipstick as he lights and blows out a match. Or the cries of a man begging a kitten to take milk; it's all of her he has left. Another narrating for me as he waits for his erection to form. Just, waits. Whether they are mute here because the spirits are sedated or because I am sedated or because all our soul's sufferings are stacked too deeply to distinguish one from another, I do not care to know.

It seems for a moment there is in all the world only me, the woman to my right, the bartender, and the man in the kitchen who she might desire. A lingering memory of this morning. But I push it aside.

I ask the bartender for a pint glass of the house white, a shot of well whiskey, and a water. While I wait, the woman two seats down looks at me. "Are you alright?" she asks.

I think about this. I smile a little and reply, Are you?

The woman laughs and sips her clear liquid through a black plastic straw, which hangs along her face like a worm. Like a leech.

The woman tells me she's not usually here at this time of the day. As she says this, the bartender calls her by her first name, which I do not catch, tells her to slow down.

The woman rolls her eyes.

I start to say I'm not judging either way, but the woman has already continued speaking.

The woman says, "My boyfriend has a custody hearing today. So, I don't really know how I'm going to get home now. He drove me out here this morning for an interview for some services or something. But. I just want to stop worrying so much, all they're going to do is give me more to worry about. You know?"

I bite my lower lip to stop myself from asking more, from inserting a path to salvation that doesn't involve a corrupt government or liberal elites or handouts from bootlickers. I nod. Drink half my pint.

The woman keeps going, "I know he'll come or he won't and it'll all keep going on. There's no reason to worry either way. But."

I nod again. I'm familiar with the agony of the wait, the relinquishment and the punishment, the dread of the confinement at the end of the wait, or, the freedom granted by loss.

Elaina whispers, Judas.

The woman appreciates my nod and nods herself, a fun house mirror.

The woman says, "Usually I'd just walk you know but I hurt my ankle on the assembly line last week. Meat packing. That's why I was in town to begin with anyways."

The woman pulls out her leg so I can see, and yes it is in a dirty blue plastic boot. The thin limb inside is swelling against the casing of a tightly bound Ace bandage. It pulses like a blood sausage. And thinking this I feel hungry, then sick again. I have an image of this woman behind animal carcasses on the assembly line. I imagine her thin arms deep inside the chest of a cow seven times her size, pulling intestines and organs and scooping. Bloody. I'm sure this can't be how it works. I see the woman multiplied and every person I imagine in the plant is weeping behind their lost animal. And also, I think of my own bloody body, the thin layer that constricts and the mass I found this morning. I swallow some more vomit. Chase it with the whiskey.

The bartender finally returns to me after lingering with the man for too long, but I can see her worry as I ask for more. Like I might become a problem. Both, I say, please. The woman to my right is still sipping on her vodka over ice; she tells me more about the accident, which had involved not just her but four other workers and a fair amount of product. I imagine the woman trapped under the body of the cow, the intestines spilled out around her, the head of the animal sweet in death. Smiling. The eyes torn out. And the decrepit woman's gummy open mouth screaming as her tibia breaks beneath the weight of the corpse, those coming to her aid slipping in the blood.

While I drink the second pint of white wine like water, turning away from the woman to my right who is frightening me, she says, "I'm two weeks late." She says it like a confession. "I'm usually like clockwork, I have been since I was fifteen." Considering the custody hearings, a baby wasn't something her boyfriend was going to let her do and his ex-wife would have a fit and—she stops. The woman says, "But, I can't kill it?" It is a question.

This is not what I came here for. I say only, I don't know it's up to you. But something about me today says it wrong.

The woman eyes me, up, and down, "You have a look to you. You're not from around here." I say I'm from New Jersey. The woman is not sure what to make of this, but finally decides to trust me. She whispers,

"You know, I can't say this to anyone, but, I don't even believe in heaven. I don't even think I believe in anything." I think that this woman should believe in something, because I think this woman has always been and will always be in hell. I think her child, if she has it, will be born into hell and will live her whole life trying to crawl out, vying against every other child simultaneously trying to save themselves from our burning earth, like crabs in a bucket.

I say nothing.

The woman takes a long sip of her vodka and we sit together for some time drinking everything we have left. She is talking to herself now, a little hysterical, "But, I don't want Jesus to see me killing a baby like that too. I don't want to see myself murder anything either." And also, "Haven't I seen myself through enough? Shouldn't it stop sometimes?" She is right. Atrocity is abundant and relentless and no justice is coming. I wonder what is *should*.

It seems to me as if the woman's unborn child is sitting at the bar with us, a few invisible cells that discontinue their journey on the countertop. Elaina's Apollo must be watching me these few midwinter hours in which he has power, a trickster god playing cruel jokes on her behalf. But this afternoon I am just looking to worship what I love and beg it for a little peace. I do not want to receive prophecy, and ignore the vision.

To the woman I say, I don't think there's anything

wrong with not wanting to do it. I don't say that I do think there's something that feels wrong with wanting to do it sometimes. It would make Elaina so angry. To admit there is some confusion to existence, that I can both wish to have never been born and think it a sin to deny someone a life. Even a life in hell. Wanting to understand things beyond us does not mean we should project our heart onto others, is what I want to say. There is more than one way to be virtuous. Then Elaina would ask me if I would deny the mother life, and I would say no. Then Elaina would ask how a society might be built without laws in the interest primarily of its citizens, and I would say I don't know. I would say maybe I don't want a society. Maybe I don't want you telling me what to do anymore. And Elaina would laugh at me, *But you are too stupid to know what to do for yourself.*

I ask the woman if she will keep the baby, and if she will raise the baby. Even if her boyfriend doesn't want it. I am trying not to think of Elaina anymore, the ice bucket anymore. I tell myself I am just thinking of this woman, sipping her vodka and picking her lips.

The woman says, "I couldn't. I need him."

The woman says, "Someone else will take care of her. I know so many folks who want babies."

I think of Immanuel.

I think of being small in a white blanket.

How did Christ feel in Mary's body when he was returned after the third day? I have a vision of Elaina's loose mind and her chattering, her cool hands around my ass and thighs.

I ask the woman, Do you truly believe in nothing? Or do you believe Jesus cares for you? Jesus was always a point of contention on the compound. Between Elaina and I. Certainly between Jesse and Elaina.

Jesus's purpose in living is to die, to be abandoned and to suffer pain we cannot fathom, before dying. Or, at least that's how Jesse would put it. And if I mentioned the holes in Christ's living hands, Jesse would flinch. Pain! Will this ordeal be true of his second body? Jesse had asked this before accepting Elaina's inquiries into his seed. Elaina said we are not Christians. We are the first true faith since the ancients! Our godling will be his own person, and, he will be both of us, and he will be the light made flesh.

But after the boy's birth, Jesse had become increasingly agitated when contemplating what fate Elaina might see for her god child. Elaina would tell Jesse he was being small-minded. Why was he bringing all this old toxic dogma to her beautiful new world.

But, to the followers, out of earshot, Elaina would say, "He is our redeemer come again." She would answer to Madonna.

I can't help myself. I ask the woman, Do you believe in the love of Jesus Christ?

The woman says, "Yes, I guess I do."

Why?

I am worried she will tell me to trust his death, but

she is more interesting than I give her credit for.

The woman, "Because of that volcano back, oh—"

Were you saved from a volcano?

The woman, "It isn't that kind of a story."

I am out of drink. I am hoping I am wrong and the bartender is not in love and will return and be attendant and generous and remember she is a woman like us. Sometimes women in love act like they are better than the rest of us. But if she is not in love, she will see us both together clearly needing more drink, and she will offer it up with ease and empathy.

The woman says, "I have a story but it might offend you."

I say, I won't be offended.

The bartender sees us and is in some half-state of shared consciousness and brings me more whiskey, but I have to ask for the wine, and she does not bring the woman the vodka she will want when she is finished with what she is thinking about. The bartender's long painted fingers are brushing back and forth.

The woman to my right, "It's kind of a story about a whore. The whore who fucked that man who died in the volcano? That Henry man?"

I say I haven't heard of him, that I didn't even realize there were volcanoes around here. The woman sighs, too tired to walk me through all the local history.

The woman says, tapping on her boot, "Well there was, and he did. This man Henry lived all alone on a little ridge near the lake. He'd gone crazy after killing his first wife so he could be with her younger sister. Drowned her in a lake. The older sister, I mean. The first wife, I mean. And then after Henry had the sister he really wanted she up and died a few months later. I think that's the story. And this whore would go up there and drink a Coke with him and slip down her panties and pretend she was both of the wives together." The woman thinks. "The angry one. And the sad one. Which I guess—"

I know, I say. Elaina had explained to me the primacy of certain emotions.

The woman to my right, "She just must not have been that good of a whore though, if that was her kind of man. She was pretty enough. You understand?"

I say I do. The woman gives me a once-over, and decides despite my appearance this afternoon, I must have at some point. "Well Henry is the only one who died in the volcano. He wouldn't leave his house; he said he didn't trust the government. Really I think he wouldn't leave his second wife's ghost. But we were all scared we were gonna—I mean I remember it as the scariest thing that could ever happen while you were still living. I mean, from what I knew then. It rained ash for days. You couldn't see the sun or anything."

I would die to keep the memory of the times when Elaina loved me. I would boil inside my casing to remember the feeling of her small lips around the tip of my finger in the early days, to hear voiced the first song she sang to the newborn god. Thinking of it my heart seems to move further into my body. My breath is shallow.

The woman to my right is frowning.

The woman says, "When the volcano erupted, my mother was sick." Pauses. "My mother was friends with this whore, only she didn't know her friend was a whore, and the whore didn't know my mother was sick. And the whore was staying with us in our trailer to keep safe, out of the blast zone. The whore lived by old Henry remember so she couldn't really stay there or she'd be burned to a crisp. And we were all just playing cards and drinking and waiting for the ash to pass like it was a snowstorm or something. Drew the shades. Pulled out our rifles. Like my daddy thought maybe the volcano would come knocking on the door." The woman breathes in through her nose.

The woman says, "And then there were two men who wanted in. Soldiers who'd gotten lost." Her eyes are faraway.

I want the woman to return. I am lonely when she is in memory.

I interrupt her reverie, And you were all okay in the end?

The woman shrugs. "The whore shot one of the soldiers after he tried to rape her, after he'd finished with me, and my mother died of the cancer a week later and from then on it was just me and Daddy, and Daddy's friends..." The woman thinks. "But what do you mean by that question? Were you just wanting to know if we turned to crisps like Henry?"

I say, Yes, I guess that's all I meant.

We drink.

I say, So why does that make you believe in the love of Jesus?

The woman pulls her straw out of the ice of her empty drink, chews on it, "Well—it is as simple as I believe in Jesus because my mother did, and told me that's what kept us safe. And maybe I'm not so sure about him for the same reason.

"I hardly remember her anymore except every morning before school she'd brush my hair. Fifty times on each side. Pulled it tight into little tails. Sometimes even I'd bleed." The woman is quiet again, then— "There's always something new, isn't there?"

This was of course something that would directly lend itself to activation for salvation. Nuclear holocaust? Climate apocalypse? Fascist empire? Micro-biomes? AI takeover? Elaina, on her highest highs. *I have borne the living inheritor of our father who art in heaven's kingdom. Believe in me! Do not doubt my calling and all shall be as you've been too afraid to dream of.* Come join our flock. Come, finally, home.

But I am not Elaina. I do not interrupt the woman here, merely agree with her. I do not offer any kind of a solution. What she says is simply true.

The woman looks at her stomach.

The woman says, "If they touched me, so what? I wouldn't do that. I wouldn't let anyone do that."

I do not argue with her.

It is interesting to me that in this woman's story about a volcano, the bits of it I was able to gather—rock, lava, cumulus black clouds, the Earth itself—had not entered into the story. Not even the town that might be demolished, or the plant or animal life that would be forever marred by this eruption which the woman has alluded to. An incomprehensible splendid terror which was brought forth by a source that had lumbered in the earth for eons, and continues to lumber beneath us. This eruption that lives inside this bar through the memory of the bedrock of the town itself. All these things were a quiet and invisible backdrop to the main narrative. This core that the narration rotated around was less consequential than even the most vile of its human victims. The woman, telling her story about the wild and beautiful terror of Earth, was only capable of talking about herself. Although she could tell her intimate relationships were not the only thing of importance, she had no language to share with me the greater context she could sense, even in her mention of that small-minded, radical, Jesus Christ.

It is only recent and Western industrial tradition that insists people only care for themselves. Individualism's recency makes me optimistic. I want to tell the woman to be hopeful, that maybe our culture will be wiped away, erased by revolt or some sweet surrender to the natural world. But I sound like the followers, and I do not know, with this woman, how to begin.

The woman is looking at her drink anyways, and doesn't seem interested in sharing any more. I think to myself, I could last another hour without looking to see if the blood has stopped. I think I can give myself that hour as a gift. At the bar the body is a buzzy stranger I've dissociated from. I cannot even feel my toes. I cannot even hear myself swallow.

The bar is properly opened now and the televisions begin humming. Local news. National sports. The voices as they enter the bar, chattering about nothing, make me feel so much less lonely. I almost start to cry but I don't want to be seen yet. I want to last as long as I can in a liminal space of knowing, and not being known.

The bar is playing a song I sang to Elaina sometimes. It is a silly melody about a teenage girl and the older man who wants her. I used to laugh as she reached for me. I can see the bartender singing along and it makes me think of Elaina touching me while she hummed and my legs rub against one another and I am so far away and for the first time in many weeks, I smile. The smile hurts my jaw.

When it is over there is another classic rock staple. It too is familiar enough to sting with all the blurry memories of every time I've sang along with one I loved. The times with Immanuel.

A couple walks in the bar. A tall woman and a shorter man.

I whistle a bit of Immanuel's echo song with sudden inspiration.

The woman looks in my direction.

On our trip West Elaina and I stopped in Oklahoma. We stopped in Michigan. We stopped in Nebraska and even dipped down to Arizona. Sometimes when Elaina would be frightened by a spirit, or receive a whispering from the lord, we would make a sudden car chase kind of U-turn. Then drive the car for days in the opposite direction, until she again was overtaken by another sense.

I had never traveled through this part of the country. My life had been small, geographically. A childhood in Jersey with my schoolteacher mother, child support payments from my father who we never saw after that incident when I was nine. Before my mother's death, she lived in the same small house we grew up in, alone for all real purposes until her death.

I started modeling at fourteen. Moved to the city. Until Elaina suggested it, suggested there might be something real for us, I'd never left. Before her I'd liked the way almost every experience I'd had, every mean-ingful moment and person, could be charted like a map onto the city's blocks—like gripping a Heineken and bickering with the bartender at Ruby's on Coney Island on a rainy day, the way I'd seen my partner do it, and my uncle before that. I'd think, Maybe this is the most we can hope for, to see some lineage or inheritance, to be held, if not physically, then in this way.

Georgette when she came to us had nothing in life but a boyfriend with a studio apartment who left hickies and rope burns on her long neck. Hunched shoulders. Acne. Her minimum-wage job.

Georgette blossomed on the compound, her skin cleared and she took long walks among the foxes and deer which eased her tense muscles and brightened her eyes. She stopped smelling of grease and smoke and instead bathed daily with a soap Martha made from kitchen fat and lavender. Georgette knelt nightly at Elaina's feet, asking for stories.

Elaina loved a young mind, because although she did not want to admit it, I believe sometimes she thought there were some for whom it was too late. Did Elaina think this of me, that at nineteen I was too far marred for her caresses and lessons to do enough to alter me to a form that suited her? But also, who would I have become without Elaina's influences? Whoever that person was, she would not have been worthy enough fully grown to capture Elaina's eye. Elaina desired potential.

In the beginning of her second year with us, Georgette became enamored with a carpenter who would do occasional work for us. Our Joseph of course. Our most beautiful tool: Jesse.

It is only thanks to Georgette's love that Jesse came to us.

When Elaina was just beginning to try, she had so many conditions to the conception. I think she was for a long time truly expecting the sun to impregnate her on its own, and maybe I was too. She would lie in the hot rays, her taut waist unmoving. She would ask me to pray over her for the child she sought. And I would move down. And she would cum into my mouth.

We were all so much younger then. I remember feeling, for some time at least, that we were finally safe. So far north along the Idaho panhandle that we could run to Canada on foot in fifteen minutes or less. Should we ever need to. No earthly force could separate us from one another, nor from our faith, which was fresh and new and strong. The followers were eager to meet the god they had been promised. The god Elaina had promised to bear for us.

When Georgette brought Jesse into the fold, he called her his little rabbit, even in public. He wore marks from her cum along the bottom of his shirts. Jesse was fully Georgette's before he was Elaina's. Georgette who was something like a daughter to Elaina, her lover too. Always eager to offer herself, with a wide face and freckles. And she brought Jesse to Her.

When Elaina announced she was pregnant, finally, with the savior she had been promised in her visions, Jesse was standing next to me, the cuck husband, in the crowds.

Georgette, upon the realization of our risen savior's parentage, left our flock.

When I think of the early days, how good it could have gone, I think of Georgette dancing in Jesse's arms near a fire. The way the small of her back arched under the length of Jesse's hand which allowed her beneath it, freedom. Their limbs joined in a furious red aura against the comparatively calm yellow of the fire, or the pinks and greens of the dying day on the horizon.

12 P.M.

Elaina loved the stars as a child. She said her relationship with the sun felt portentous, urgent, even in
youth. It was only at night she felt unburdened of this
connection. She would lie on her back on a hill behind
her parent's trailer park, counting until she could not
anymore.

Elaina gave each star its own unique name, developed her own constellations. She knew the eons
between them and within which an incomprehensible
galaxy was overflowing with its own mass of Elaina
variants, other conscious beings looking down and
watching her and entreating that she rise up and meet
her potential. But these beings, being like her, were
gentler than the sun—Elaina told me.

Elaina told me this about herself one of the first
nights we spent together, still entertained with me, her
prize-winning sow. Those first days she would fuck
me stupid, and then while I lay in bed stunned by the

absolute and eviscerating submission of the experience, confess to me. Made object I was allowed to see the unvarnished truth of her, and I devoured her tales. I begged to be abjected more.

Elaina said as a child, watching the heavens, she'd sensed not just the Christian God's presence, a lesser god, but the first god of Ra, that initial heat which all life still turned to and obeyed. She knew then this heat was her soul connection, the only thing worthy of her worship. She did not know to keep this truth quiet at first. As a child of seven or eight she'd confess her awareness of the multitudes of heaven to teachers at school. Friends' parents.

Men were the only ones who would listen to her. In closets. In locked spare bedrooms. In cars. Their fat sweaty palms on her knees, thighs, up. But, she could not be penetrated, she told me. The spirits would not allow these shaky appendages entrance. She said her flesh burned them and the countless observing selves protected her with their light.

She told bishops and priesthood leaders of her visions.

The holy men in their suits with their hands not just on her naked knees but her elbows and shoulders and neck—who tried and tried to claim each of her cavities for themselves—explained yes. Her father in heaven was waiting for his princess to return to him. The men promised they could help her understand. That Elaina, especially, was poised to understand. If she continued to be such a good girl. They could explain it all to her.

The men said, You shall be as the heavenly mother herself.

The men said, You shall be the lord's greatest tool.

Elaina said she would leave the rooms with the men and lie on that hill, when her father had gone to sleep, and the stars, the selves who inhabited their body, would multiply even as she blinked. She would feel the people of the Earth walk towards her too, ready to touch her body and feed from it. Suckle truth. They slipped around her and into the air. And Elaina saw all the million Elainas who were like her, who attracted and repelled in equal measures their own stars. The souls trapped in their own gravitational pulls.

I could see Elaina the child, alone, swarmed by want, her invented want which allowed no space for victimization. I saw the Elaina I'd first known in films. Her nipples. Her white lace and the tufts of her under-arm hair. The white fur around her belly and back.

Every night the spirits would approach her. All the businessmen in Tokyo. The scientists in the Arctic. The celebrities on the magazine covers, and also the people who took their photos, and also her mother's friend in the checkout line, and also the clerk. And also a girl who braided her hair once. And also a boy two grades younger who she had once kneed in the balls. They were all touching her body. All these spirits at once.

I asked, Not the spirits of the animals? Not the plants?

I thought of the feeling of grass on the lowest part of my back. The way earth would catch in the sweat, the hairs muddy and curled. The spark of cognition there. And I thought beneath Elaina and supporting her was of course the worms and fecal matter and decay that all these bodies would be part of.

Elaina shook her head.

Elaina, *We are not of the earth, baby girl. We are of the heavens. You love something that does not care enough to love you back.*

Martha said her husband was taken by a spirit.

Martha said the spirit could be kept away sometimes. If he took his medication, if he kept away from drink.

Martha said she learned she had only one need, and that was to mollify her husband's spirit. Her husband's spirit was not her husband's soul, the soul of the man she had fallen in love with in middle school, who was kind to her when no one else was, who reached under her 3XL T-shirt one day in a parking lot and said she had the best tits he'd ever felt, who would roll her joints then pull down her pants, sit her on his lap in his car, make her wet and warm and full and wanted. Her husband's spirit was not that man. Instead her husband's spirit was a strange demon which possessed him if she did not work hard enough to keep the thing at bay.

Her husband had asked her, when she was a girl and he was not yet her husband, *Martha, can you handle my darkness?*

Martha worked as a maid in a motel, and a dishwasher at the downtown pub, and sometimes sold plasma or welcomed the neighbor's children in her home for a little extra. Martha spent her free time cleaning and cooking for him and the boys, and also tried once to take in her sister's infant who was born addicted to meth. The baby's soft skull in a little blue helmet frightened her, so she wrapped it in a ribbon. But she was not allowed to keep the baby for long. The baby was put up for adoption and taken in by lesbians in Oregon. When Martha had a few hours to herself she would play Halo with the sun blocking curtains drawn. She would take the OxyContin she'd been given by her coworker's boyfriend.

Martha's husband, when the spirit overtook him, would sometimes leave the house. He would sometimes return in a few days, sometimes in a few months. And always when he came back he wanted. He wanted money and he wanted Martha, the way she was when she was young; how had she let herself get so fat? So old? He wanted the apartment filled with the things they'd dreamt of in youth. They had said they would be better than their parents. They'd said their children's lives would be happier. He wanted their sons to behave and he wanted time with them and he wanted them to leave him alone and he wanted breakfast and he wanted to sleep in and he wanted the fourteen-year-old who lived at the end of the neighborhood to show him her perfect tits and again he wanted Martha, but not

Martha as she was. Why was Martha who she was? And the spirits would tell the husband to demand this of her. Against a wall. But Martha could not answer when forced, could only insist that if she could breathe she could try to find a better answer for him. For why she was the Martha she was, and not the Martha he wanted.

For a few weeks on our trip out West, Elaina and I were snowed in at a motel in Laramie, Wyoming. One of those strange suspended nights, I snuck out while Elaina slept and looked at the stars for myself. As I looked, I thought of the girl-child on the hill. I thought of all the lovers who had looked at the pillars of creation from afar, and all the people like me, alone, who were sure we could feel less so through attempting to comprehend our insignificance.

I did not feel the joy or peace Elaina expressed her child-self experiencing. As I looked at the sky, I felt nothing but sadness. I felt only the solitude of life, not the expansive closeness I'd experienced upon leaving the city. I felt only my pull towards Elaina, not the pull of the heavens or the earth or my own heart or body, but only a tethering to Elaina's needs. Only Elaina's spirit, loud in my ears. Wanting.

I looked at the stars that night, arching as if the slope of the planet could itself be comprehended and touched, and I contemplated the fiery bright pit of the Orion Nebula and the blissful elimination of the sin-gularity, and I pulled back. Although I had sought the

stars to escape her hold on my mind, every phenome-
non instead returned me to her. To wanting her.

I was always trying to explain this to Elaina. That her
love made me emptier. To feel connected to anything
on this Earth the way I was to her, specifically her,
meant to demand that both of us be recognized as
special and apart, which is both a lonely place to be,
and a false one. I was trying to explain to Elaina that
I think I am not different from anyone else, that we
are punished, that I want to stand with my brothers
and sisters in this punishment. We are suffering,
heartbroken at the warming summers and the thinning
ozone and the death. We are rejected as we have been
abusive, even without understanding our violences.
The Earth is turning away. Is expelling us. We grieve
but deserve this rejection. All of us together. For her to
ask me to love her was for her to ask to fundamentally
reject this truth, and also to invite more loss.

I tried, despite myself, to explain some of this thinking
after arriving back at the hotel. I tried to tell her our
love must be bad, our attachment misplaced. I should
not care for her. I should care for the foxes and the
leaves and the wind. She was free to love all mankind,
why was I relegated to this selfish desire for her alone?
Elaina was not asleep when I arrived in the room,
prepared to make some sense of my thinking, but
instead sitting upright, eyeing with wrath a square foot

of wall near the door.

I was afraid of her, but still I sat beside her and tried to explain, pointing at the stars outside of the window as I did so.

Elaina, frustrated with my constant disagreement, my argumentative nature, my uneducated indefensible frustrations which I was incapable of scaffolding with the appropriate logic, life experience, patience, asked me if I did not believe in her and want to devote myself to her, then would I mind telling her what it was I thought I was doing here.

How could I explain how, before Elaina, I was an individual existing among individuals, albeit a small one circling small ones, paddling through the spaces we'd stolen, but that after her I was just Hers. I became this willingly because it is what she required of me, but the loss of the rest of living was a great sacrifice. Greater than if I'd slit my wrists to feed her with my blood. Greater than if I'd sold my soul, whatever such a cheap vintage could be worth. That my body would never respond to touch again the way it did to hers. That she had ruined my own body. That she had separated me from the greatness of shared experience of community of the land, even of the spirit. Those days if I closed my eyes it was only—

Elaina said, "What do you think you're for."

My body responded with arousal.

Elaina sat cross-legged and erect on the bed, and her small lips were pressed together in disdain. She shook her head. Sex would not mollify her. She drummed her fingers along her knees and upper thighs.

Elaina said, "No."

Elaina said, "Give me your faith."

It seemed cruel to me that love could not be enough. If this is love, this consumptive state of terror. This chronic disposition of observation. I loved the way crowds would part to allow Elaina through, both the admiration and fear of the people. I loved her twisted optimism, her assuredness. I loved watching her in conversation, pulling strangers to her view. I loved that she was the bravest person I had ever met. I loved the way Elaina gave me release in bed, that she chose me to understand so intimately—that full and visible transcendence she gave. That she was the witness to my transformation. I loved when she allowed me to return that pleasure, and when I was allowed to witness her stumbling across the edge of herself and into the greater consciousness. I loved her sick mind. I loved her because she was so aware, and so unselfaware. I loved the way she could not take a joke.

I knew Elaina only loved me out of desire, or need. She liked my body and devotion. She liked the way I looked in the city, trailing behind her and holding in my cupped palm her elbow. I would provide her with these things as long as she would allow me to. I would minimize myself, I would diminish.

But, I could not provide her with faith. A final

corner of my mind resisted, and I resented it.

As we sat and spoke, the Earth moved. The trees grew. Animals slept or shat or fucked. The Orion Nebula, and all the unfathomable wonders within it, danced. I sat next to Elaina on the bed and reached towards her, and away from the world.

The couple in the bar stands out. Too ironed. Too healthily robust in the arms and thighs rather than the middle. The man is stiff. I am familiar with the ways those who think they understand the holy interact with the sinning. Those secure in their relationship to other realms are not like this. It is only those who are afraid of losing something, who deep down are unconvinced of their convictions, who flaunt their hard won halos.

The woman is more fluid. She moves towards me as if being pulled. She hums a little of Immanuel's song in response to me and I do not cry. I do not.

The new woman says, "May I have this seat?"

I nod.

The storyteller to my right is sticky in my consciousness. I tell myself I hardly know if she is dead or alive, like she has not decided herself. And this new woman is lovely. She is freckled with fine light brown hair cut around her chin. When she sits, I see her hands are thick and ribbed with cords of muscle and veins. I sip at my wine and hide my shot glass from this new woman. The man companion sees this as he takes his seat.

I listen to the couple as they talk. Their car is

broken. Where will they get it fixed? They will call the Elders who are in the area, Do you still have their number? I have their number. Just let me get something to eat and I'll call.

Their righteous purpose in this space is nauseating.

I was right about the bartender. I can see the man in the kitchen letting a hand linger on her body as she passes. And the woman to my right is on her phone with her boyfriend, negotiating the terms of a ride. He is on the other side saying sorry, I'm sorry.

I might not be able to contain the memories or the want or the anger.

The echo song is running like a chant in my mind.

The last of the dead baby's home leaks between the mouth of my cunt and onto the bar seat.

I can tell I am bleeding through and I cannot make myself care.

Especially if there is another drink.

Is there another drink?

I notice suddenly, and it comes in a wave. The woman to my right smells. Her unwashed boot is putrid and now that I have noticed it the stench intensifies my own sensations of self-disgust. The juxtaposition of the perfume and deodorant on the too-groomed couple to my left.

Gnats congregate on the rim of my pint of wine.

The woman to my right looks at me with big soft eyes like we are the same.

Elaina's voice whispers, You didn't want to see what

she looked like?

I think of bouncing Immanuel on my knee.

I think of Elaina in the doorway, a doorway of an imagined house which I have painted gold and green. If the seed were hers. The doorway hers. If the gods had given us the tools to fulfill our love. And in this fantasy, Immanuel was mine too and peering at his sister's face. Not toddling always to Jesse. Not sensing their sameness.

I am whimpering a little now, I can hear it but also cannot stop it. It isn't crying yet. It is something stranger and more distasteful. The woman to the left, with the big hands, looks away from her husband, assesses me, places one palm on my wrist and one on my back, and begins an attempt to soothe me. She is telling me, Shhh… shhhh honey. She asks me if I'd like anything. I shake my head. I reach for my wine but can't quite grasp it. The woman hands me her full glass of water. I pull the cold glass to my lips and can lick at the condensation but cannot tolerate the taste of the liquid's purity. I feel the woman to my right looking on at the scene. She is envious.

It is catching the scent of this woman again that makes me stop my moaning.

I do not want to be like her.

The woman to my left tells me I look exhausted. I tell her I'm fine. I'm not from here, just tired from traveling. The woman gestures to the man she is with, who is frowning deeply. "So are we." The man cares for this woman's interests and asks me, "Did you come here alone?"

I say, No. My husband will be here soon.

The woman to my left says, "Okay."

The woman looks at the man she is with. There is a little bit of an ask in the look. I can see the woman is so beautiful and kind and the man is so enamored with her that he will do anything she asks. But she, I see, is in return required to never ask too much. I resent that she can gracefully toe this line.

The woman to my left asks me, "Do you mind us sitting with you while you wait?"

I shake my head. I feel like a child suddenly. She is benevolent. I am beholden.

The woman, to the man, "I think we will have time…Why don't you go call the Elders?" And, "Yes, I know, but I'm starving. I'll order something for you. It won't be here for a minute. What is even here?"

I want to say, I am here.

I try to say, I am here.

How can a thing both be here and not?

Elaina whispers to me, "You're starting to get it, baby."

1 P.M.

On the compound in the winter the trees were stripped
of their branches and the shadows hung long against
their bodies. Georgette said she felt bound by them.
Pulled in.

This is a skill Jesse was gifted with. Binds and knots.

One evening, as I heard from Martha, as Martha
heard it from Georgette herself, Georgette lay hogtied,
her white flesh cold and bruised, and Georgette asked
Jesse a question.

Georgette, "Jesse. Do you like me?"

In response, Jesse told Georgette a story about his
first wife, Mary.

Mary was tall, like me; willowy, like Elaina; gentle
and serious, like Georgette. Mary was monied and
Mary was cultured. Mary had come from the city, but
Mary preferred the long fields near Jesse's stone based
cabin. Mary had a white cat with matted fur and green
eyes named Fern who she carried about on her arm like

the lady in the portrait with the ferret. She wore her dark blonde hair in pioneer braids. She did not like to sit too low to the ground on account of her long legs and stiff knees.

Mary and Jesse made love for nearly ten years. Almost always in the same fields, in the sunlight, with Jesse lowering Mary to the ground, a hand around her head and a hand along the length of her back, Jesse helping her back up the same way.

Mary would cook a large stew once a week. Bake bread. And Jesse would make her little delights. An omelet. A slice of cake. A cup of espresso.

Jesse met Mary buying sugar, eight bags of it, at the local town's grocery. Mary had a cart with a faulty wheel and she clanged it against Jesse's, saw his wire full of sugar, and blushed deeply as if she had walked in on him exposed, or been told a dirty joke.

When Mary joined with Jesse, she brought her goats, her hens, her herbs, her tiny hand stitches. They slept in a tall four poster bed and Mary never once allowed him to turn away from her in the night.

When Mary became sick, Jesse would tuck stray hairs into the dark little crevices of her braids as he watched her sleeping on her side, the wrists, just bones, pulled tight against her. Occasionally limbs slipped from the side of the bed and Jesse would pull them back towards her while wrapped around her body. She left him her land, and he sold it ten years later, when offered the distraction of Georgette's adoration and

Elaina's vision.

On the compound, there were feral cats Jesse would startle at. Would curse at. Until he began to collect them and systematically eradicate them. Tomboys and calicos and litters of kittens. Who knows how he did it. Some suspected he was like Elaina, impartial to earthly pain, that this was her draw to him and that he would torment the cats by slowly breaking each tiny bone. Or drowning them and listening to their high-pitched purrs. But some said, No, he is her foil, he must be merciful. Snap their necks.

Jesse had spent the five years after Mary's death in almost complete solitude. Surely, the congregants would say, the man was a deeply feeling human being. Not a monster. Not another god.

The kittens had kept the population of the bunnies in check. By the time Immanuel was born and Georgette nowhere to be found, the compound was overrun with soft little bourgeois ears. Rutting shaking blurs.

The story of Mary was the only answer Georgette ever got to the question of whether or not Jesse liked her.

I once asked Elaina if she had been hurt. If there were things the spirits had not been able to protect her from. Places in her body where darkness had found a way in.

This was in our early days when I would crawl into her bed and for days would not leave, would beg her not to leave. I would cum sometimes just by a kiss. She would run her tongue along my nipples and clavicles.

She would whisper secrets to my stomach. And I would spasm.

After one of these days, I asked Elaina if she had been hurt. I was washing her feet for her. She was never warm, so she would often submerge her purpling skin in hot water, and as she did this, I would massage her calves and the soles of her feet to help the blood return to its cycles.

I don't know why this is when I asked her.

Elaina did not care to know about my own hurt. She did not want to hear about my father's heavy hands or my mother's light-swallowing grief. The schoolchildren who cornered me and a young boy in the gymnasium one day, made me suck his flaccid cock, both of us crying. My first boyfriend. The photographers. A stranger on a train.

I said to Elaina, Is there something you're not telling me?

Elaina laughed at me and stood in the tub, the steam rising up around her person.

"You think a mortal could harm me?"

In the early days, Elaina liked me to join in her games. Before I grew older and more sullen. Before I knew more about her than she had decided to confess.

In the early days, Elaina often asked me to watch as men took her from behind. Rough, up the ass. Hands around the front of her neck and in her mouth like a bridle. She would not scream. Nor moan, nor arch or squirm. And she watched me throughout. To see how I might respond, if I had less control than her.

Occasionally she would ask the men to take me too. I did not like the pain, but I was also too proud to ask them to finish when she was there to witness, and so would endure for as long as they might want to last. Sometimes whimpering or begging, but never receding from the experience entirely. When the man would cum inside me or on me or on Elaina or in a cup or around my hair like a halo or a web, and after the man would dress and close the door behind him, Elaina would rise from her seat in the corner of the room.

Then Elaina would place her face between my legs, and so gently, kiss me better. Clean me with her tongue.

When she did this I would cum so hard I thought I would die.

The taste of her approval. So rare. So intent.

"And to discover this now, when I'd thought I would never be happy."

The woman to the left of me at the bar had been speaking for long enough that I felt lulled, drawn in and out of my memories, and hers. The woman to my left, while as verbose as the woman to my right, was so persistently pleasant as to be speaking in an entirely different tongue.

I marveled, as the woman to my left spoke, at the small wrinkles near her eyes and mouth. So soft in healthy, plush skin. Like they were pointing somewhere. The woman to my right had tried to listen for some time, too far away to really hear us, but then her boyfriend called again. The woman to my right tried to say goodbye to me and I nodded, but could not meet her eyes, delighting in the glowing attention of the woman to the left's peaceful ease.

The woman was describing to me her conversion to her husband's faith. She first told me about meeting her husband, their early life together. And though it was tender, I had to fight boredom at the simplicity of her life's ordeal, even as I appreciated the pleasurable veneer of sweetness. Before him I knew there were darker truths she was keeping from me. She would allude to them but would not depict them in her words, which were chaste and tame. Her voice very low and a little raspy and her hair fluttering out, like she wants truly to run and fuck. It is a strange juxtaposition, the holy language and a body that seems under the top button, to want.

I recognize that without the woman to my right as a point of contrast, I am now the most disgusting body at the bar. Elaina is keeping me from admitting why I am so weak. She is telling me if I focus on her memory a little longer, drink a little more, I do not need to see the rest of the day.

The woman to my left, "Sitting in the chapel with my husband's family that day I felt such a strong sense of belonging. Like these people see me truly, and love me truly."

I nod. Martha in particular had expressed a feeling
of unique satisfaction at being incorporated into the
fold. That she no longer needed to worry about herself,
how she was perceived, the way she or her sons might
face prejudice. Martha said, "Like letting down a load I
had not known I'd been carrying."

The woman to my left, "His mother would embrace
me. She would sing every hymn in the wrong key,
loud—and she would laugh when I did the same. His
father was a convert too, and he explained to me how
strange it had all seemed when he first was baptized. I'd
never seen a family so in love before. I'd never known a
life could be full of one emotion and one only, joy.

"Can you imagine that? A life of joy? Just joy?"

I say she cannot possibly feel only joy, but I do not
know why I am attacking her conviction. She takes it in
stride, but as if to confirm her own hyperbole, giggles
and places one of her strong clean hands on my shoulder.
I feel how dry it is with the winter air. I feel how clammy
my flesh is beneath it.

The woman says, "Of course you are right. Even
now, I am a little sad about the car. I am a little worried
my husband does not love me as much as I love him. I
am a little nervous you find me strange. But, these are
small things. Everything of this Earth must pass. But
families are forever. Love lasts for eternity."

The woman presses her lips together and hums.
Full octaves. It is true she is like her mother-in-law and
cannot really hold a note for long. I echo her warbled

hum the way Immanuel would echo mine with my own soft voice. The woman again begins to giggle conspiratorially. I think of Immanuel toddling around the compound or gripping at my fingers. I gasp, thinking of the ice bucket. I cling to the woman's forearm, afraid I'll fall off my chair.

But the woman is engrossed still in her own story and does not notice the change in me. She is subsumed in the sensation she'd had that day of being accepted and loved. She says, "If you follow the teachings of Jesus, there was and will only ever be joy, only love and joy."

The woman to my left, "Even as I feel any discomfort, I know it is small compared to the endless lifetimes I shall live in the hereafter in the eyes of our lord and how I shall be loved eternally. And how I shall be warm be warm be warm for always."

Joy joy joy joy. Joy.

She is talking so fast she has yet to even have a sip of her drink. A Sprite with ice.

I say, Please, I think I need help getting to the bathroom.

The woman to my left notices my full appearance, my face which is wet now with mucus and tears, and pulls a little at my touch. But then she comforts me again. "Of course, of course."

I attempt to push myself off my chair. If she will not offer me help I will not ask for it. Her husband walks into the bar and sees me struggling as I am and calls to his wife, "Claire." And she looks to him and then falls a little out of her trance of memory and turns also to me and it is as if she has seen me for the first time in a consolidated state.

The woman says, "Oh, baby." But she says it with a little bit of disgust.

I say, Can you help me?

Some spirits have snuck into the bar and are laughing.

Why are they so often laughing these days?

Like Elaina the woman is confident, secure that she will provide me with whatever I need.

The woman grasps the left side of my body, supporting it under the armpit with her tall shoulder, and her husband takes my right.

The woman to my left, "Honey, where do you need to go?"

2 P.M.

Jesse walks into my hospital room and tries to smile.
Fails.

He was never very good at reassurance. Elaina did
not need him to, she required nothing of him but his
body and its product.

Jesse tries again to smile.

Jesse smiles.

It makes me a little sick to see him like this.

The room is white and small, a geometric-patterned
curtain between my bed and the patient in the bed next
to me. The patient on the other side of the curtain is a
woman and she is moaning and screaming at the staff.

The patient, "I have been waiting hours for you all.
I've been here all day! I want to see a doctor I deserve
to see a doctor!"

The patient, "I am hurt! I am hurt!"

And the whole ward can hear she is.

Jesse's never-smile does not slip, but instead sticks and holds. I must be so terrible that he must protect himself from me this way. I try to make myself small enough to be easy, and always I fail critically.

I have not been crying. Elaina has taught me not to cry so well, but somehow there is water in my eyes and on my face. Jesse is smiling, and now I fear he is not smiling to protect me, but instead because he is happy. I wonder if my loss means finally we are all even. The gods have been paid.

Immanuel does seem to be in the room with us. Sitting calm as he often did, golden in the light, counting the seconds in the silence between verbalization and verbalization.

One, two, three, four—

I grab at the bottom of Jesse's shirt, use it to wipe my eyes as I pull him closer and say, She is in the hotel. They keep asking me where it is to bless it and give it a funeral or to see if it was me who did it and I will not tell them. And they are angry. I say, I am afraid.

Jesse lets go of the smile; he does not like my admission of fear. It melts halfway down his face. It pulls into his skull.

Jesse sits on the edge of my bed.

Jesse says, "I will not tell them."

I need him but I do not trust him. He is a mortal no different than me.

Immanuel would call him this and laugh, imitating Elaina when she was angry. *Goddamnit, Jesus fucking*

Christ Jesse. Immanuel, looking at Jesse, *Mooooor! Cackling at the joy of the sounds that were smashed together. Kkkkkkrrrrmooor—jesusfuckingchristjesusfucking moooor!!!*

After I fainted, the woman to my left at the bar and her husband put me in the backseat of their car. The woman, whose name is Claire, was flushed and talking fast. "I had no idea you were in so much pain! Just blabbering on about myself like that!"

I tried to explain to Claire that nothing was wrong with me, really, I was just missing someone. It feels so bad but they tell me missing someone cannot kill you on its own. No matter how bad the missing feels, you cannot die from it. The husband gagged as he removed his hand from my bleeding body, looked at the chair covered in blood. "Claire honey, I think we need to take her somewhere."

I said, I am not alone.

I fell, then was transported, then woke not to Claire but her husband who told me only, "We've notified the elders and they will be here soon."

I nodded like I understood. I said, I need—but he did not hear me.

I sat for what felt like a long time in the bed. I was cold I was hot. I did not know if anyone would come for me or where I would go. I had only the few bills left from the bar in my back pocket, but I did not know where my pants were. There was no one left but Jesse who would care for me, and I knew that, at least for a day or so, I would not be able to take care of myself.

I lost vision in one eye.

Behind the curtain, the patient screamed, "I'm hurting!"

When a nurse entered the room I reached for her and said, Please, I am not alone.

It seemed to me the nurse sneered, but she allowed me to use the phone to call the motel and Jesse answered. I told him where I was, and when he came he was smiling that fake smile, it seemed for my benefit, and now I have ruined everything and made him sad again.

The patient, "I'm not waiting here all night! I'm not an animal! I'm dying! God, if they won't help me with the pain won't you! God, please!" She laughs.

I sense the spirits from this morning have returned. But they all belong in a children's ward I think. Toddlers and ten-year-olds with long red hair and even one infant, loud in the corner. They are all calling out to me for things I cannot give them and my pulse is at a fever pitch. Why are the spirits laughing even here? Why is the patient?

Elaina was hunting for the right property online, and I would laugh at her. She called me a luddite, I called her a youth. But when we arrived at the cabin she'd found on Zillow, with the dreamy green acreage so far north, Elaina said, "This is the place." The blood was pulsing close to her flesh.

When she said this, I was compelled by its truth. I ran my hand down her skull, cupping the base in my palm. Down the back of her neck. The rocks mimicked the shape of her body. The water outlined her shoulders, the small divets of muscle in her upper arms.

Elaina moved away from me, and I let her.

The cabin was big. An oddity. Octagonal and two stories with every wall covered in floor to ceiling windows. The sun sparkled along the floors. It would cost us the last of Elaina's money after the divorce, her second husband I never asked after—although as I began to know Elaina's unspoken secrets, I knew by her avoidance of his name that he had inflicted significant damage worth the price she demanded.

You could see the glorious temple the cabin would become upon even that first viewing. Elaina walking through the rooms, slow, like she was in a wedding processional, spinning a little with her arms outstretched. Beckoning towards the people you could envision blooming around her with funny moustaches and rain galoshes, or in bare feet with hairy calves and exposed breasts. All sun-kissed. All glowing and warm and sated. And the furniture too seemed to bloom around her with that easy optimism of an empty home. The table here. A wine rack. Hand-carved wooden chairs facing the window. Plants and animals and gold vases for yellow flowers. Plush rugs and handmade quilts. You could see the followers in their costumes sitting and laughing as they watched the sunset. Glasses tinkling. Or, gathering along the stairs whispering to one another while Elaina cleared her throat to speak. Touching each other's knees and ankles and waists, both with fraternal and sexual intention. And I followed Elaina as she walked through these throngs of beings yet to be, and then out the doors, and took off her shoes, and padded softly along the dirt, eventually kneeling, sinking her hands into the moist earth.

You sometimes forgot Elaina was a woman. All angles and ferocity. And then she would become mother so quickly. A maternal icon. Elaina sank her hands into the soil outside the home and I thought, She loves me.

I walked towards the lake.

I put my feet in the cold water and felt the sharp sting. Insects were skittering along the surface and in the mud. They pierced my flesh with their mouths and I relished this sharp clarification. I thought, Finally we have somewhere real. Finally we belong somewhere. You do not ask to believe in something. It is like love. Belief chooses you.

I walked deeper into the lake and a small fish grazed my calf. Another. A small school and I closed my eyes, turning my cheek to the hot sun and sinking deeper into the mud.

Elaina splashed in behind me, laughing and rinsing her hands. Seeing the fish around me she scooped some into her hands and raised them to the sky. They glittered silver and the water drained from between her fingers but the fish remained until she relinquished them down into the long transparent bands. Gills and scales and fractured light and states of matter I could not comprehend folded together into a shared space.

I kissed Elaina's cheek and she pulled her palms deep into a fist with a kind of ecstatic rage, each knuckle bent too sharp the water still clinging to the white skin an illuminating shroud.

She pushed these fists against my ears.

Elaina, "God is all over you."

I felt this to be true then.

3 P.M.

Elaina and I would often spend Sundays in Prospect
Park. A delight that became habit, that became routine,
that led to the end. One of these Sundays, an abnor-
mally warm winter day, Elaina was drinking coffee
which had long ago turned cold. Her sentences were
moving in their usual incessant loops—about the
colors as she saw them, as if I had never seen red before,
or green, or yellow—the emotional impact of each
shade upon her. Every dead language she was uniquely
proficient in.

Elaina had this habit of staring directly into the sun
while she spoke, which was striking us through the long
shadows of the trees. Already he was pulling her in, and
their relationship cracked. I remember she would touch
my body as she spoke. A delicate row of knuckles on a
knee. The tips of her small cold nails behind my ear. I
wish to believe she was truly with me in those times.
That the love I felt was not a reflection but a bond.

I, blessed by Elaina, Elaina, blessed by Adonis, were approached by a brazen five-year-old in a pink fedora once, his mother chasing some ways behind him. The child asked Elaina if he could take her photo with his disposable camera. Elaina laughed and consented, leaning back in her fur-lined leather jacket. Turning her bald head even further into the sun, so it shone wet like her eyes. I'm sure there is some term in Latin for the impact.

The child was able to acquire two photos before his mother arrived. Both with Elaina in the same long-necked posture. Both with Elaina glittering. Not just her winter flesh but the silver along her ears and neck. Her buttons and belt buckle. Elaina said an old Celtic blessing for the boy when he walked away with his mother. Elaina smiled. Elaina told me the boy reminded her of someone, with his serious affect and his broad face.

I asked Elaina who.

Elaina pulled herself against my body, pushing me backwards along the picnic table, her hot head sneaking beneath my shirt and against my flesh, her cheeks to my stomach. I laughed, delighted and humiliated as she burrowed deeper, her shoulders pushing up the shirt, her face between my breasts, until I pushed her down and out.

Straightening myself Elaina placed a hand on either side of my face, pressed her forehead to mine.

Elder Fitz is from Idaho, not the north where we'd built our home, but the farm country of the south. Wet hay bales and cattle and root vegetables.

His companion, Elder Mond, is from Utah. He says in the town of Orem, where he was raised, you cannot walk down a single street without seeing a church or temple of the Latter-day Saints of Jesus Christ. Elder Mond says that God is matriculated into every aspect of his saints' lives, so that when you are cradled by the mountains, which rise up on either side of the valley in which Orem and Provo lie, you feel a confirmation from the Holy Spirit that God's hands are manifested in the landscape, and you are among the Lord's chosen people.

Elder Mond is talking about his home too long, I think. Elder Mond might as well be saying, I was safe but now I am afraid. I see Elder Fitz is calm though. He was never cradled in his faith, but had to build it.

The two very young men are half-illuminated by the slits of yellow overhead light over the top of the curtain where the woman is still yelling. The staff will not attend to her pain, and she will not allow any of us peace until they do. Which seems right. My bed is so dark. There are no windows.

It was wise, Elaina thought, for the sun to not always be present. Elaina thought that for the protection of her follower's immortal souls, she must not be among them too often. Night served a function. Want exists because it cannot always be sated. Desire is a product of withholding. Elaina would have laughed at Mond's valley because there was nothing more grotesque to Elaina than a satisfied body. A wet body. A safe body.

I was at first so ashamed of my slick cunt at her slightest movement. She forgave me but she wanted me washed before, during, after. She would watch me wash. And if she was unsatisfied, she would wash me herself. She would insert enemas. When we were the deepest in our desire, we would scourge our bodies of all waste and excess and then she would fuck me for days, neither of us allowed release. Until I thought, surely one of us will die from the want. But no one ever dies from wanting. That's what they tell me.

I would always surrender first.

The followers were indeed moved to deeper devotion in the darkest hours of the night, during Elaina's ordained fasts of light. Some began to withhold sunlight from themselves, from their children. They would do this for penance or out of a desire for admiration. To prove their worthy righteousness. And when these individuals were gaunt and pale, Elaina would appear to them. And forgive them. And lead them to the light where the golden orb would produce round drops in their eyes.

Elder Mond is the picture of health. Elder Fitzwater too. Both are trim and tall and clean, but not too clean.

They have showered today but they have not changed shirts after sweating through the afternoon. The hospital's smell of metal and piss cannot completely obscure the male musk.

They are young enough that I see Jesse with them and I startle. How have I come to be in the company of a man so old? I remember that Jesse is older than my father, and that I have not seen my grandfather since he was around the age Jesse is now. Jesse runs his hand over my forehead and skull and down the length of my neck, like he is smoothing the hair of a child. I lean into the hand like a cat and Elder Fitz blushes. Is he aroused or is he embarrassed for me? That I am contained like this.

Elder Mond holds out his hand to Jesse, who moves it from its graphic position on my body, and the two men shake. Fitz does the same. I am not offered a hand.

Elder Mond says, "Hello, my name is Elder Mond." He points at his name tag and then at the second man, "This is my companion Elder Fitz." Jesse nods and says, "I'm Jesse and this is—"

He looks at me. This impediment, which is usually a sweetness, adds to my terror—that he cannot find the words for what we are.

I say, I am his wife.

Elder Fitz says, "It is wonderful to meet you both."

Jesse has made me so afraid with this pause. I am conscious I do not have enough ways to say I am afraid, nor articulate the density of the fear, and so seem redundant in the repetition of my thoughts.

Jesse says, "Are you boys visiting rooms in the hospital?" They twitch slightly at boys.

"No, we were asked to come here by a member of our church, our Sister Claire Morgan. We helped her and her husband with their car troubles earlier today, and she expressed that we might be needed here as well."

I tell Jesse Claire is the woman who helped me get to the hospital. Jesse says, "Thank you, I'm just not sure what—" "I can handle this now."

Elder Fitz is still trying to look at anything other than me. It makes me very conscious that I am naked under the hospital gown. I am conscious that the very nature of my stay in this room, the condition I have found myself in with my still-inflated stomach, is inherently sexual. Is, perhaps to a boy from a farm in Idaho, very sexual. That childbirth may be a reminder of silky bodies penetrating and responding. Even hollowed out and breaking I fear I am object for others, not even object itself. Elaina teaching me history. Women who are bayonetted and raped in alternating turns by marauding soldiers. Anything phallic an arousal.

Jesse feels me thinking and puts his hand again on my forehead. I cry out at this touch, just a little, and despise myself, but I do it. I yip like a little dog.

Elder Mond finds his courage, and asks to sit at the foot of my bed. I try to say no so Jesse offers Mond his chair.

Jesse climbs into my bed and moves me against his chest. An almost reversal of our pose this morning.

Elder Mond, "We are so sorry to see you in this situation. We feel we have been sent here to do you a service, to tell you the truth of a God who loves all his children, including you."

The missionary hands Jesse a small card, and a copy of a book of scripture. Jesse looks at the card. On one side is an image of a glowing Jesus Christ, palms open to the masses bearing clean center wounds. Before him kneel brown people in feathered headdresses and beads. On the back of the card is a quote. "Behold, by and by ye shall pluck the fruit thereof, which is most precious, which is sweet above all that is sweet and which is white above all that is white, yea, and pure above all that is pure—and ye shall feast upon this fruit even until ye are filled, that ye hunger not, neither shall ye thirst."

I see Elaina walking down the streets of Spokane with Martha's sons.

I see fire.

Elder Fitz, "Maybe when your wife is finished here, we could give you a ride to wherever you are staying? We can ask Sister Morgan to join and share some more of our message?"

Jesse does not say no, only, "I can drive."

Elder Mond, "Of course, whatever is the easiest for you. We are also happy to help you get food, or procure a resting place for the child. We want to be of service."

I pull closer to Jesse, my nails biting the skin under his T-shirt.

Jesse, "I have money—" (A lie.)

Jesse, "I can take care of my own. Thank you."

He is exhausted and I am enormous. I remind him of them. Every day.

Where will I go?

Elder Mond, "Then maybe all we can offer you is the truth of this scripture, the Book of Mormon, a truth of Jesus Christ in the Americas which was given through prophesy to the young man Joseph Smith. We offer you the knowledge of a living prophet, Russel M. Nelson, who receives revelations from a Heavenly Father who loves us, to guide us through these lonely modern days. We offer the atonement of our Heavenly Father's only begotten son, Jesus Christ, and the promise that your sins can be wiped from your bodies through his sacrifice."

Elder Fitz, "Maybe most importantly, we can share with you the true knowledge that families are forever, and that there is a life after death full of fulfillment."

Elder Fitz pauses as if he is relishing the message he shares. Then he continues, "—fulfillment and joy held by the ones you love, who we promise not even death can part you with."

The woman in the next room is screaming.

Fitz and Mond are quiet, arms folded. Fitz's head is bowed slightly while Mond watches Jesse receive this information with reverent wanting.

Jesse is sitting too still.

The woman is screaming. Why will they not help her with her pain?

Jesse gives a low aching hum, which becomes one of Immanuel's songs. Someone's in the kitchen, I kno-o-o-ow. The fields at dawn, the touch of sudden rain on the front porch, the three of us eating a morning meal. Immanuel standing at a too-tall table drinking from a full glass, tiny hands shaking at the bulk of the vessel. Immanuel following Martha around the kitchen, Immanuel's call to Jesse—*Esssssssss*. A high-pitched warble as he ran from one end of the porch to another, always colliding home with Jesse and I. A pile of love.

I think of Elaina asking me while the neighbors fought next door, Truly, does God forgive? And, Maybe I have not done it yet.

I moan a little and Jesse looks at the elders, then turns to kiss my hair.

Jesse says, "Quiet baby—" "I want to hear what they have to say."

4 P.M.

Jesse and I would refer to Immanuel as "our man," the way he would saunter through camp. A confident walk with jutting stiff legs and eyes only for what was ahead of him. He would move away from me this way, then turn, *You come too.* And I would say, Whatever the man requires. Once after spending a day outside the compound watching trains I could hear Immanuel babbling in his room, *Mama Mama and the trains.* And then singing a little. Our echo song.

Immanuel would run to me when he was hurt or upset, more often than anyone else. He would run to me and I would embrace him and hold him and tell him it is okay to cry. You are safe here. And I supported his neck and held the weight of his head as it threatened to drip backwards away from my shoulder. And I tried not to weep as well. I thought it would not be good for him to see me weep as well.

Elder Fitz says he met Carol when he was seven. Her family was from West Virginia, but only a week after her mother's death from lung cancer, Carol's father drove the two of them up to that small Idaho town, Fitz's town, where the father bought and managed a Motel-8. A magnet for truckers and vagrants and all sorts of socially neglected oddities. Elder Fitz fell in love with Carol the first time he saw her in their grade school class, stripping the tip of a pencil with her teeth which were dark with lead. He would visit her and the men who orbited her life. Would sometimes talk to them about the long stretches of black road, the existential angst of a life lived always in the night. Their hunched shoulders. Their porn. And Carol would sit with him while he talked sometimes. And Carol was too pretty by half, Fitz thought.

Carol was nine and as tall as her father, a short balding Pentecostal who would shout his devotion at the skies when he could not find a proper space of worship. Wave his delicate fingers. Wiggle them. It was Mormon country, just north of the Utah border. But the mountains were too far off to see and there were none of the safe fences Elder Mond had bragged about keeping the Lord's chosen people contained and protected. Just dirt roads and hot gold fields. The memory of the promised land.

Elder Fitz said that growing up the church had seemed pointless to him. He envied the truckers for their spiritual phantasms on the road, the two dotted lines looking more and more like parted legs. The way they talked about the stars. The aliens. They seemed more complex and real than the stories he heard in Sunday school. He even envied Carol's father, the evident depth of sensation that came with his loud lamentations in the nights. Elder Fitz thought it seemed as though the man's skull dripped blood just like the Christ's when he was fully engaged in his rages to the divine.

Carol would also visit Elder Fitz. She would come to his farm often to talk to his ma and sisters. While they cooked, she would help take care of the babies. Elder Fitz followed her around both her space and his, and so he learned not only about the ways of wild lonely men, but also of the strange domestic tasks he had previously been spared. He learned his mother ate throughout the day in stolen morsels, chopping things to bits on the side of the stainless steel sink—even though she professed at dinner that she did not need. He learned the tighter you swaddled an infant, the less it would cry.

Elder Fitz, "I wasn't devout."

Elder Fitz, "I hadn't been baptized yet and only knew the church were to my mother as breathing. The scriptures like food or water. I remember believing that my prayers were heard. I knew for certain when I knelt by my bed at night that I wasn't speaking to thin air. But that was about the extent of it all. Carol took a liking to my family though, and wanted to learn more. She had

questions I couldn't understand; she took to the gospel
so naturally, like she'd been waiting her whole life to
hear it. I didn't know enough then to answer her." He
sighed here. "She needed me and I didn't know enough
to help her. I couldn't tell her then that her mother was
there on the other side, waiting for her. Because I didn't
know it myself. But maybe if I'd told her she wasn't
alone, she wouldn't go looking for company from that
man if she'd—if she'd felt some comfort before —"

I think I know where this is going and I think of
the pubescent as prey, as someone who was too good
to last. And I see the Pentecostal's Lord of hellfire and
ashes tell him his daughter was dirty. That she had
grown a fondness for filth. What do we do with dirty
things?

"I was so angry when they took her. Hurt her like
that. When my father walked me to the baptismal font,
and dropped me into the water, I thought they can
never take this anger from me. I was so ashamed I could
not save her, I thought, *No water, not even no God, can
clean me.*

"I felt the water against my skin and I felt in my
wrath myself pushing against it. But it spun into me.
Into my pores. Into my lungs. It was taking everything
that I thought was me and I felt like I'd been under a
bed of coals, like my bones were finally in their right
sockets, and I thought what is there left of me who
is this, even though I was only eight I thought this. I
thought, Are they taking the things I remember about

Carol? I remember being scared. I couldn't even hear the blessing spoken I was so hot inside the font. Then, cold, like they'd taken even the heat I'd built from my body. I was called then to bring peace to all who needed it. I felt the Lord speak to me and say that I was of the tribe of Ephraim, as was later confirmed by my patriarchal blessing. I am here on this Earth to spread the word of the Lord, to tell people that they don't need to suffer. They aren't alone. They can all have the peace I—"

What purpose could anything offer that was greater than servitude to a holy calm? What cost was not worth it?

The Immanuel in my mind watches the passing trains.

"I wish I could have told Carol she didn't need to be afraid. I wish I had given her the peace of knowing it would not last much longer."

I said, What won't last much longer.

Jesse suggests, hopefully, "Life?"

Elder Mond inserts himself here. "The grief, Sister." Looking from Jesse to me Elder Mond says, "He speaks of an end to the missing."

Jesse's body feels flushed against mine—burning, like he too is engulfed in icy flame as the young Fitz was in his holy font of blessed water, green with mold and chlorine, and rising from it in a state of immolation.

Immanuel watching trains and sitting on Elaina's lap.

Immanuel sitting on Elaina's lap as she turns her

head over her shoulder to look at me. She mouths, *What sacrifice is not worth restoring God's love to his people? What price could be too high?*

Elder Fitz, "This is my testimony. If you turn unto Christ and accept his consecrated pain, you yourself shall never feel the hell of loss again."

5 P.M.

Jesse walks the elders to the lobby to discuss the evening
to follow, while I remain in my hospital bed, rolling my
head forward and back to see if it is still attached to my
neck. To see if it still throbs or if my mortal shape has
abandoned me.

The spirits have found me here now that I am alone
and awake, and they are mocking me. Teenagers and
other equally afflicted and youthful sprites.

The spirits, You cannot control your own man?

I try to explain to them he is not even mine. He is
someone else's and we are just condemned to hurting
each other for eternity. But these spirits are too young to
understand this kind of relationship.

I miss Elaina.

It feels like a betrayal to miss Elaina more than I
miss the child that had been inside of me. But I know
that when the elders were talking, Jesse and I had been
thinking of the same face. Immanuel's. Elaina's perfect

face inside of Immanuel's face. We were not imagining our own baby, and it should be a gift to me that I would never know how much less he, and I, would love the child made of our bodies with no trace of hers.

If what Elaina asked of Jesse was selfish and cruel, what I ask of him might be worse. To live forever without her, but with the memory of her, and our crimes, embedded in our every shared moment. Jesse had reminded me the week before, his palms against the wood of a side table while I spoke in circles my fears. *You are the one who came to me! This is not my fault!* His hands gripping my shoulders, my neck, both our veins pulsing.

Jesse screamed, *This is not my fault!*

Elaina had been offering up animals since the beginning. Does. Bucks. Then does and their fawns bound together. Whose bodies were burned to completion, wasted meat and hides, leaving only piles of antlers and hooves and a few black bones. At first this was a ceremony which would end her instated fasts. An infrequent occasion followed by more feasting.

But later, it occurred whenever Elaina craved it.

I think sometimes she did it when she was lonely.

Not that I could fault her.

The spirits are still laughing at me. They tell me I have lost control.

I tell them, There's no joke here. I never had any. I never did.

Before my father left for good, there were many

anxious evenings watching my mother hover at doors or windows. I would put my sister to sleep then sit with my mother as she drank through glasses of tequila cut with grapefruit juice. Her confidences when our father was away were so adult, and sometimes after drinking she would grow unusually observant of me, even doting. This night she told me I was a beauty, that I was almost as pretty as she was when she was young. Before my father, with all his promises.

One night, sensing some power in this dynamic, I asked my mother a question I had long been wanting an answer to. I asked her what love was.

My mother placed her hands in her lap, the L of one hand meeting the L of another. Index finger to thumb. And she touched her fingers like that for some time. And she told me, without malice, *How could I explain love to someone who will never be worth it.*

I can hear the doctors in the hallway having conversations. One nurse has just been dumped, again. Her coworkers are huddling around her, crooning with feigned compassion. A doctor barks at the crying nurse and when she is gone, they twitter behind her back. About her old insecurities, her suicide attempt the year before. One of the pack, bored with the gossip, comes to check on me. She does not make eye contact but instead checks my pulse and IV. Says, Probably another hour. Says, Do you have a ride home?

I see Jesse enter over the nurse's left shoulder and

she catches his shadow and watches him walk. Yes, he is still beautiful at twice my age in ways I will never be considered again. The unjust loss of my only power is crushing. I do not want him to see this nurse's watching eyes. I want him to come to me to brush the hair from my cheek with his hands like I am Elaina.

The nurse, leaning towards Jesse. "As soon as you finish your paperwork, you two should be ready to go."

Elaina would demand the nurse speak to me directly. Elaina would place Immanuel on the chair behind her and forget him. And he would be reading a book or looking out the window or threatening to jump off something too tall. And I would say, Elaina watch out! And she would turn around just in time and the nurse would condemn us both, but Elaina and I believed we were not small women the way we believed the nurses to be. And we would laugh at their feminine anxieties.

The nurse on her way out to get the papers touches Jesse's shoulder. Whispers something to him. Jesse looks at her, at me. He is sad. I think if they talk to Jesse they will say society must charge him for the death that stalks us.

I say, Please don't go.

The nurse pulls Jesse's hand and he follows her.

When my sister died, I asked Elaina if she had known.

Elaina would not look at me.

She drank water.

That day clouds hung so low. The orb behind
it creeping and the fog was woven with thin little
strands of water and earth. I asked Elaina, Why are you
showing me the veil? Like, if I cross it, will I be given
some kind of freedom?

Elaina said, "Freedom?"

Elaina laughed. "Baby, what does a word like that
even mean to you?"

6 P.M.

I visited him once, my sister's husband, a widower with
their young child.

The son was quiet and the contained masculinity of
the husband's small house in the country illuminated
my sister's feminine qualities in his young person.
Her blonde curls and long lashes and legs. I wondered
sometimes how her husband could even bear to look at
his son without thinking of her.

I could not help but feel some relief at her death,
which Elaina dismissed as proof of my monstrosity.
But, I knew my sister so well. I knew her enormous fits
of pain. I knew the thin line which separated her from
the heavens. Even her husband knew her aura towards
the end was pure white and that she had always danced
easily along the fissures of the ethereal, that she longed
to move on. I saw these angelic qualities in her son.

So, it was only upon her son's death, a respiratory
infection he could not shake, and my sister's husband's

subsequent suicide, that I expressed the tantrum grief
Elaina had wanted to see in me. I asked Elaina, Why do I
deserve this?

Elaina's labor took five days.

The water broke, the plug popped, but no god
appeared.

Elaina asked only for a locked door. We set up a
small inflatable tub in one of the main cabin's back
rooms. But for five days, the god child would not come.
Jesse stood in the corner of the room when I returned,
stoic, watching the blood and water roll along the tarp
floors.

When the baby rolled out of her body, too long and
not purple and mewling but a healthy tomato red, alert
eyes, a fully formed small man, Elaina looked a husk
of a woman. A crone. So much so that I worried she
might not make it. And Immanuel only smiled and ate
from her chest while she nodded off. I was awed that
he held such power over her. I became afraid that she
would resent him forever for being the one thing she
could not control, and that one day there would come
a reckoning.

In the car, Jesse tells me we have been invited to dinner.

It is hot in the Applebee's. The elders are at the table
with Claire and her husband. They beckon us.

I haven't yet eaten today but the smell of grease

makes me feel sick. I want only to lie down but Jesse is stern. I fantasize about the slow death of starvation. I think of the girls I walked the runway with who were too diligent in their work, and crossed some invisible line. Jesse fingers the plastic around my wrist. He orders for me. He presses water into my hands.

The hospital gave me adult diapers for the blood and pads for my leaking nipples. When I first saw the milk I screamed, What is happening to me, and the nurse who had been talking to Jesse felt her way around him and came to me and said, Hush. "It is a natural response to the body craving. Your body is ready to feed your baby." And I howled.

As if compelled by my screams, the woman the room over also began to shout again, and then another man in a far corner bellowed and the spirits began again their laughter.

Jesse asked me why I was crying and I put his hand to my leaking breast and he flinched, pulled back his arm. Disgusted.

The patient, "You have to help me! I am a human being!"

The nurse looked at Jesse, eyes wide, then me, then the curtain, and Jesse came to hold my shoulders and press my body and limbs down. Jesse covered my mouth, we listened to the patient. I was proud that the patient would still demand humanity when I was so stupid to so easily do away with mine.

And now we are at Applebee's.

The cupped padding against my breasts is rough along my nipples. My ass and cunt are coated in a similarly silky polyester cotton. I am all oozing orifices. All mortality and sin.

Jesse is still fingering at my hospital bracelet like it is a cuff.

The elders have already ordered. Steaks and potatoes. They douse both in butter, sauce, ketchup, gravy. Claire and her husband have salads with chicken. Jesse has ordered a molten lava cake, a grilled cheese, fries. He is trying to tempt me but he is hungry himself, devouring. Elder Fitz offers me some of his steak, "Do you need the iron?" Everyone is drinking Diet Coke and water. I ask the waiter for an iced tea, a red wine. I need it to alleviate the burden of spirits in this place.

I have decided I will try to make the spirits my friends. I find I am in need of friends—but for now I need just a little quiet. All the voices here are hungry.

Jesse shakes his head at me as I order. He is afraid of my drinking. But I persist. I pour five packs of sugar into the tea and clink the ice around the bottom and begin to alternate sipping at it and the wine. Soon after the voices and the nausea ebbs. My cramps are slower. I feel strong enough to have a bite of the cake, two fries, and this mollifies Jesse enough to leave me be.

Claire is whispering in her husband's ear. She offered me a heating pad in the waiting area of the restaurant, used felt lining over the plastic body, and has not looked directly at me since. The berth offered

reminds me of the one I gave the meth addict at the
bar. Like certain griefs might be transferable through
proximity.

I wonder what has changed for her? I wonder if she
is trying for her own child, if she is newly pregnant. I
wonder what kind of suspicions of catching my inhos-
pitable state she does not want to admit to harboring,
or if I am uncontainable now it is known to all I was
incapable of hosting life. I again think it is grotesque
to have your sexual history shown so baldly on you
without your consenting to its visibility. Is she afraid
that I am beautiful? I was and might still be. Is she
afraid to see me with Jesse, jealous? I am finding myself
very funny today.

Full of beans—we would say of Immanuel, running
laps around the kitchen, the fields. His best days. And
our best days were always his.

I tell myself, Baby, you are full of beans.

There is a family with a toddler at the table nearby.
Perhaps Claire does not want me to notice? Or, does
she simply not want to think of her own losses.

Before we ate, I thought the elders might cross
themselves like Catholics but instead they fold their
arms gently, one over the other, rest them against their
chests and bow their heads and say nothing out loud. It
is a form of prayer I've not seen before. Nothing like the
loud gestures we offered to our gods. Our lover. Our
son. Our prayers were a party. Elaina hated the quiet. I
asked them what they were doing. They said they were

just telling their father thank you for the feast. Claire smiled at her palms. "He's felt so close today."

Of all the roles Elaina filled in my life, mother of course being one of them— she was not matronly in prayer. She was terrifying. I stroke the cool heating pad on my lap like it is a cat. Claire asked to be seated at a table near an electrical outlet so I could use her little gift, but I do not want to give her the satisfaction of showing how it soothes me. Better if she does not know. I watch her face out of slitted eyes and stroke and sip my wine.

I am thinking of Elaina's prayer still. Like she was some male servant of Zeus or Dionysus. Something masculine and delightful and epic. Nothing gentle like these innocent small boys. Mond's tie is pink, I have just noticed.

Claire is eating her salad in small bites. Mostly just the chicken. Her husband has finished his. The elders are scraping forks along their once-sizzling platters. Elder Fitz ate his steak first, Elder Mond his potatoes, and now they are either finishing what is left or savoring what will crown the meal. Jesse has eaten all the food he ostensibly ordered for me, except for a few fries. He pushes them towards me and I shake my head. The waiter returns and I point to my empty glass, More wine, but Jesse places his hand around mine. Engulfing and muting it.

Jesse, "They'd like to—" "Can't you wait?"

When I was younger, sometimes I would incite in

men a desire for possession, and sometimes this desire
would make them stupid, and sometimes it would
make them accommodating. I look at Jesse and see how
much this day has aged me.

I look at Claire who sees what I am attempting to do
and asks for the check.

Her husband pays.

I say to Jesse, Are they coming back with us?

Jesse looks at me repulsed, but nods.

I feel his revulsion and feel satisfied that I am
perceived.

I would watch the women on the compound brush their teeth. I would watch as they washed their necks or massaged the skin around their eyes. There is such pleasure in other women's company, shared knowledge of the violence of being always perceived, until you are invisible. I would stand with the women of the compound and touch my own face, smooth my own furrows, in response to their motions, feeling such a deep loneliness. For romantic love to have kept me from sorority for so long. Elaina knew how quickly solidarity could poison.

The elders sit on the edge of the bed, facing Jesse, who has moved the television to sit on the end of the entertainment console. Claire's husband and I have taken the chairs, one on either side of the room, and Claire kneels at her husband's feet. I had insisted I would be the one to sit on the floor but the room tsked and Jesse settled me against the wood and my arms glued themselves to the railing like I was strapped.

I looked again and again over my shoulder to the ice bucket. It was between Jesse and I, and I wondered if he could sense it. I didn't want the strangers so near. I had told Jesse where it was. Did he remember? But more than that, did he feel any connection to it?

The spirits could sense my preoccupations. Loud again in the motel room. They hovered around the thing, giving the elders, and Claire in particular, plenty of empty space while protecting the container and I was grateful. I thought, Thank you. The spirits are like melted mercury and the invisible porous barrier they form could harden at any time.

Claire's eyes will not leave my body.

Elder Mond invites us all to another prayer.

Mond sees my expression and clarifies, "An invocation."

The group folds their arms the same way they did at Applebee's.

Jesse imitates the posture then looks at me, raises his eyebrows when I do not move.

I feel a little sick. I feel like, even if I am so ugly and aged, scraped out like a melon, even a little simple, is it possible that I deserve this boring of a fate? Are these childish people—not childish—children are wild, and not funny—but gauche people, grotesquely gauche and willfully naive—really be the snare I deserve today?

Elder Fitz senses my worry.

Fitz says, "Think of it as a conversation."

Mond, "A…heavenly conversation."

I grip the arms of the chair and will not move.

Jesse nudges me and I hand Jesse the heating pad which I have been carrying and ask him to plug it in. At first he looks like he will not but sees Claire watching him. Follows instructions and passes it back to me. I hold it against my stomach which is still in the process of eviction. This foreign squatter, hiding now in the corner, who has wrecked me. I will not accept the prayer but I am ashamed that I need the heat. I am ashamed that a gift from this dangerous stranger soothes me, the rejected host.

Mond, "Our dear Father who art in Heaven, thank you for the kindness you have shown us today. In such difficult weather you have still allowed us sustenance and safety, and you have given us new friendships," he pauses here, "…new family."

I swallow.

Jesse next to me curls into himself in imitation of his morning posture.

How cruel that I should both demand his protection and deny him the safety he finds here.

"Amen." Says Claire, her husband, and Elder Fitz.

For Elaina I would add my assent—but here? I will not. Not for starched white shirts on virgins. Not for vanilla little lies.

Elaina always told me when I was angry, *Baby, you*

are so ugly when you are mad, and I believed her.

Claire, after the elders are done praying, is the first to speak. "I had an uncle who had a fishtank," as if she had been called.

Elder Mond opens his eyes here. He had been sitting in reverie after completion of the prayer for several minutes, but now moves to speak. Elder Fitz, though, who is perhaps older than I originally believed him to be, shakes his head.

I heard a rumor, from Martha of course, that the missionaries are not even allowed apart from one another to urinate. To cry. To stroke themselves.

Claire, "My uncle would not leave the care of his fish to anyone. He had not been loved by our family, but he needed our family the most. He…he had trouble with basic tasks, and feelings. He never held a job. He lived into old age with his mother and his fish. Saltwater. A beautiful menagerie. He said he knew their moods. Could feel their needs with a prick of a finger in the water, or with a dream."

I love this strange ridiculous turn which the men, on all sides, are resistant to.

Claire, "Only one time in his entire life did my uncle allow another family member to care for the fish. Only once and for a surgery in the city which he could not avoid. But after just this one leaving, his worst fear was realized. His selfish abandonment. He knew from his own lived life that the family was untrustworthy, but he felt he had no choice but to leave them in the care of those he himself had been forced to rely upon.

"When my uncle returned home only a week later, five of his precious fish were dead.

"He never left the tank again, not for more than two hours at a time, and his entire life was hobbled by it. He had one love. This one love. He spoke of it often, the guilt. The shame."

I am envious this man never wavered in his devotion.

Jesse is watching me.

Claire had also been watching me as she spoke. "Sister, who do you trust?"

I want to say the fish. I want to say the spirits and the sun and the moon and the trees and the knowledge that you are swimming in time and that one day time will end, and be done with you. I want to say I trust that once Elaina looked at me with desire and therefore my life can never be meaningless. I almost say Immanuel's days full of beans. I almost look towards the corner and say something—

But Claire interrupts and looks towards Jesse.

Claire asks Jesse, "Who will take care of yours?"

Her husband touches her shoulder and back.

Claire says, "The world is a terrible place. Full of those who cannot be trusted. Who will cause you harm. But the church, on orders of our first prophet Joseph, offers a robust congregation and a priesthood where Jesse can be in touch with his divine purpose and calling. For the women there is the Relief Society.

A community of caregivers. Food. Shelter. Daycare. Like-minded friends. These men offer safety to their sisters. Joy, sister!"

I laugh. The spirits did it first, they goaded me. But yes. I laugh, and too loud.

Fitz begins a recitation over my laughter, "Come unto me, all ye who labour and are heavy laden, and I will give you rest. Take my yoke upon you, and learn of me; for I am meek and lowly in heart: and ye shall find rest unto your souls. For my yoke is easy, and my burden is light."

Two breaths.

Jesse opens his eyes and they are red and moist, and yet also he is smiling, not the sick ingratiating smile I'd seen in the hospital but something stranger. Something feminine and transcendent. A smile I imagine he might have given me had he come out of his dream this morning reunited with his husband.

What do I owe Jesse, I think.

Elder Mond looks to Elder Fitz, Claire has thrown them too far forward.

Jesse speaks now. "I had a girlfriend who was Catholic. She would confess her sins to her priest and he would give her a series of ways to pay God back. I hated it. I told her that was no way for a God to behave. To punish us for the way he made us.

Jesse, "Elaina—"

I say, Hush.

Fitz speaks again, "Though your sins be as scarlet,

they shall be as white as snow; though they be red like crimson, they shall be as wool."

Elder Mond, "Our Heavenly Father loves his and the Mother's creations, or why would he offer his only begotten son to experience such turmoil in Gethsemane?"

And again Elder Fitz, "You need only ask and God will forgive you."

Elder Mond, "Yes, you need only ask in prayer. You only need to seek out the Lord from a true place of humbleness and repentance, and He will lighten your load for you."

Claire is watching me.

Jesse asks, "What if—" "My sins—" "Some weights must be too great."

I sense a fire in the room which causes the spirits to blend further into one another. I see a stray genital here, an ear there. They are sighing with pleasure and pain. I feel the heat of the flame and I see that it is rising. The rain outside the motel has stopped. I hold out my arm and see the ash as it lands on my white arm, which grows tan like it is the last time I saw this fire.

I think of this white ash on my brown forearm.

I hold it up for Jesse to see.

But Jesse will not look at me, will not see what the spirits have shown me, and will look only at the elders. He is not kissing the toes of their oiled leather shoes, but he might as well be.

The elders are eager and ready with answers.

Elder Fitz, "Jesus's pain would not be so great if he did not know all our pains. If he did not suffer for all our sins. There is no wrong he did not feel the shame of, that he did not pay the price for."

Elder Mond, "A prophet from our scriptures, which were discovered and translated by Joseph Smith, sinned so greatly he feared he would never find forgiveness. But, he did. And Enos did not continue to dwell on his mistakes. Instead, he immediately began to pray for the welfare of others."

Jesse is humming a little and still will not look at me, but Claire remains watchful and sharp.

The spirits have nothing useful to contribute, melted, all individual experiences lost.

I am bold, I say, I don't trust your promises.

Fitz says, "Please, tell us how we can earn your trust."

Jesse says, "Baby, be quiet."

He is saying, Baby, I need.

I say, I have heard your prophet raped children under threat of an angel. I have heard your bishops are the same. I have heard your women are broodmares and I have heard you believe in the mark of Cain. I have heard you do not allow for dissent in your flocks. I have heard you prize sweetness and obedience in the face of violence and I hear you live a lie. I have heard you mark yourselves with death in your temples and I see your Jesus in the Americas. I hear you believe the people who belong on this land were wicked, and killed for the sins of their ancestors. I have heard you are influenced by wealth. I heard you are backwards. Limited. Simple. Wrong.

Claire finally looks away from me. The elders only frown.

Jesse is quiet for some time then says, "What is different here, baby?"

I say, What?

Jesse says, "Than us."

I say, Than her?

Jesse, "Than us."

The flames go out but the ash remains like snow. Like it is finally the right weather for the season. I laugh again as it falls among the spirits in all their strange new guises. Their funny shapes which together are forming new stories. The victims are the perpetrators, the lonely are the stifled. And the barrier around the ice bucket has broken so I am wary, watching it.

Elder Mond avoids my wild form, my pet heating pad, my bloodshot eyes, and speaks only to Jesse. "Our brother. You and your wife have had such a hard day. We do not want to take too much of your time." He considers. "May we offer you both a blessing to help calm you? And then we will leave you to think on what we have said?" I shake my head but Jesse nods. Takes my hand in his. Implores. I look to Claire.

I say, I will only take a blessing from her.

Elder Mond corrects me, "Women do not hold the priesthood. They have instead been given the gift of life-making, of motherhood."

Elder Fitz affirms, "We all have different roles to play on earth, which we chose before we were born. Claire's spirit does not want the priesthood."

I think of Elaina taking it from behind. I think of her son ravaging her body, drinking from her chest while her followers crooned.

Claire's husband smiles, "Which is the greater gift, though? Leadership or motherhood? I sometimes wish I'd made different decisions in the premortal realm, so as not to be head of the household all the time."

It is the first time he has spoken in the room, and I realize he is maybe both stupid and bored. I wasn't sure which, but it is both. Claire does not smile, but Jesse does. A big smile. I wonder what Jesse would have been like if he had been born into this cult. How happy he might be. I think of Jesse nursing a baby with the kind of seeping gentleness he can sometimes be capable of. Of this stuttered speech and his smile, smaller, natural, looking over his big breasts at an infant.

I do not like penetration. It sometimes hurts, but mostly it startles. Mostly I feel at the end of it that I have been made a fool of, as if someone has made me defecate in a concert hall.

Elder Mond can see my pursed lips, can see me glaring at Claire.

I want her to be better than this. Elaina's memory scolds me, *Misogyny.*

Elder Mond says, "I have something to read. It may help."

Jesse nods and the spirits are laughing. They are playful. They are amused.

Mond gestures and whispers to Fitz and the two boys shuffle in their bag. When Mond has found what he is looking for, a laminated sheet of paper in his scripture bag, he smiles. Rolls up his starched white sleeves. "I think this will help." Mond clears his throat.

Mond reads aloud. "We, the First Presidency and the Council of the Twelve Apostles."

Claire whispers beneath him, "The apostles serve the prophet." It makes me sick that she should be so desperate for confirmation of her goodness. And so sure these men, these boys, are so much better than her and can prove it. I feel vomit in my throat and tensed jaw and swallow. My mouth is dry and the flavor lingers.

Without the sound of the storm, there is quiet outside the motel. No birds. Just a little night wind which you can see as it whistles, traveling across the wild winter state. The spirits are still hovering but are in communion with one another, not us. Speaking in hushed tones.

Immanuel watching his trains.

We would build him tracks.

They would go in circles.

We would lie cheeks to the floor and watch models of his favorites go around, and around. And I was never happier.

I look at the floor and there is no Manny the man,

but there is ash.

Elder Mond nods at Claire and smiles as if to a child. He restarts.

Elder Mond says, "We, the First Presidency and the Council of the Twelve Apostles of the Church of Jesus Christ of Latter-day Saints, solemnly proclaim that marriage between a man and a woman is ordained of God and that the family is central—" Elder Fitz mouths, *Central, central, central,* "—to the Creator's plan for the eternal destiny of His children." Claire is also speaking under her breath, Central, central, central—

"All human beings—male and female—are created in the image of God. Each is a beloved spirit son or daughter of heavenly parents, and, as such, each has a divine nature and destiny. Gender is an essential characteristic of individual premortal, mortal, and eternal identity and purpose. In the premortal realm—"

Claire says, "You should have explained the premortal realm."

Jesse says, "We understand enough."

Elder Mond continues, "Okay…so spirit sons and daughters knew and worshiped God as their Eternal Father and accepted His plan by which His children could obtain a physical body and gain earthly experience to progress toward perfection and ultimately realize their divine destiny as heirs of eternal life. The divine plan of happiness enables family relationships to be perpetuated beyond the grave…The first commandment that God gave to Adam and Eve pertained to their potential for parenthood as husband and wife."

Elder Fitz is blushing.

Claire is radiant.

I am humiliated.

It is as if Adam and Eve sat between us. Eve being poked over and over again with a long thin phallus. Crying. Begging us not to look. Shouldn't the divine be divorced from this animal rutting? Elaina drinking a white load on her knees.

Elaina says, *But baby, you are the one who loves the fowls and the beasts.*

I say to the elders, Why was Mary a virgin?

Claire bites her lip and her husband takes her hand. Claire wasn't one in her wedding dress then. Divorced trash. No wonder she is groveling. The husband tries to speak. Fitz is looking at our tousled bedding. Maybe they can all smell my cunt from this morning on Jesse's unwashed body. They want me to be taken and silent about it. They do not want to see the evidence of my sins. They do not want to hear my thoughts on Jesse's sins.

Elder Mond does not answer my question.

The spirits are trying to explain the occurrence to me. They ask if I can imagine the divine ghost turning itself into a corkscrew like a duck's cock in order to find its way into its maiden without consent or damage.

I ask, Did god fuck Mary?

Jesse turns to me, "You're being disgusting."

I ask again, Is this not what we are discussing?

Jesse holds his hand up to my lips. One finger.

I radiate with the fire from earlier which I have feared, which I have not channeled. I've always been so cold and consumed with these shivering feelings of want. I've never pressed out upon others so greatly. Sitting in this circle, as if the heating pad on my belly has brought the heat of the memory of flames. A spirit's lips sealed to another spirit's balls. So many lips and eyes closed. They cannot laugh anymore; they cannot tell me I am wrong.

Elaina, *Baby. If you are not wrong then I am not wrong.*

The spirits who can, laugh.

Elder Mond rushes the final portion of his reading. "Parents have a sacred duty to rear their children in love and righteousness, to provide for their physical and spiritual needs." I feel the way Elaina looked towards the end. Did she think she could cure herself of being told what to do by telling others what to do? I think of Immanuel. I think of Immanuel I think of Immanuel. What do these men know of me? I will hang them from piano wire if they say his name. They will freeze. Elaina was wrong. I do not care for the trees anymore. I will pull them all up by their roots. I will watch every man starve for breath.

I think of the ice bucket.

Jesse breaks. Harsh sobs by someone without practice with them.

The spirits, the ones who can, laugh at him.

I am ashamed, but I laugh too. I can hear the yo ho
ho and the scraping of Martha's spoons in the kitchen
and the feeling of Elaina's hips moving to music when
she would pull me close to her and I would be so afraid.
And Immanuel is speaking to me. Immanuel says, *Ma
is home,* and the heat in me breaks like waves on the
shore, and I clutch at the felt of the heating pad. There
is no fire, I was mistaken. I am cold again. The spirits
pull apart blue and stoic.

It is cold again.

Elder Mond shakes his laminated sheet. "We warn
that the disintegration of the family will bring upon
individuals, communities, and nations the calamities
foretold by ancient and modern prophets."

Fitz is watching me.

I look to the ice bucket.

Claire implores me, "Don't you see what we are
offering?"

I finally do. And, I nod.

I remember promising Jesse a god. I could not give
him that, and so now he has found his own. Elaina asks,
Don't you think we are all gods?

Jesse says, "Baby—" "Baby, they're just telling us—"
"Oh, baby. We will be home again."

Elder Mond lays his hands first on Jesse's head.
Claire's husband holds blessed oil on his keychain
in a small wooden vial. He places three drops of the
consecrated liquid onto Jesse's scalp. The three men
stand around him shoulder to shoulder so I can barely

see through. The thick palms are all stacked over one another upon his head. One set of palms, the next over, the next over.

When they come to me, the suffocation has some relief to it.

We are not pretending anymore.

As they press their bodies around and against me I can smell their odor and laundry detergent and the grease clinging to their ties from the restaurant. I can feel the husband's sweat in particular. His palms are particularly fat and the moisture of him runs down and along my hairline. I open my eyes and can see only their groins.

Elder Mond says, "Amen."

Elaina's memory is so bad, I wonder what she even remembered of the early days. If she remembered any of it.

I wonder if she would wake some days and not know what was missing. I wonder when she looked at my replacements, Georgette or her girls or perhaps a paramour more her equal who completed the tasks I completed for her and would lie in her bed with her and worship her, if she would maybe accidentally reach for them looking for my body. My response. Maybe just once?

I wonder if it could be easier for me one day. Like maybe one day I will hear Elaina's name in conversation and think to myself, Oh, I recognize that from somewhere. Or see a toddler running and think only, How sweet. But this is a dull glimmer of a dream.

I am hunted by wanting. Every second of every minute, by the way the left side of her mouth would rise before the right. By the feeling of her against my body in the morning. Her childhood memories have overtaken my own in the forefront of my thoughts and instead of thinking of my own mother or sister I think primarily of her father. Her wanderings.

I know Elaina. She could forget even the color of my eyes. She could forget the words that came from her own lips. She could forget the acquiring of the property. She could forget those slow first years. She could forget the failed after failed attempt, she could forget the childbirth. She could forget her violent depression after the birth. She could forget the years Martha kept threatening to leave, and she could forget ceding to her will. She could forget she needed us too.

And she could forget the promises she made.

And she could forget the meals shared and the hours and that my mind is made now of her books and ideas and the ways she taught me to move and desire and hold myself among her peers. Her gentle tender touch. Her touch could be so so gentle. True gentleness requires awareness of its opposite. She could forget my youth at her hand. Our life in the city. She could forget, I believe, even the sun itself were she convinced to.

But I am made of Elaina. I cannot for a second forget her.

I hope for the beginning to return, and to take the rest of it on a different set of tracks. To once again touch her body and feel her attentions. To once again watch Jesse and Immanuel running towards me. Tripping. Catching themselves. To exist not at all and to be consumed by the lives of these loves, buried, suffocated, made nothing but soil for their stems in these moments of beans.

A spirit says, If you submit to the blessings, you will no longer be alone and individual in grief.

When we took to the road, Elaina moved from beyond my grasp, to beyond my comprehension. In the car she would offer me such sparse information, a sentence here or there every few miles, and the sentences were always prophesies.

We left the city in late March. It was snowing.

The sky was bright with sun and the trees along the side of the road black and green and pink with new growth when a sudden flush of white ice from the sky enveloped us.

Elaina gasped. "Like a baptism."

I drove this stretch, the windshield opaque with white cliffs on either side of the highway, without breathing, and when the snow had passed, pulled suddenly to the side of the road to vomit. Water and coffee and the blue undigested coating of two Advil.

Elaina watched from the car. She did not offer to hold back my hair. She did not pat my back consolingly or croon the way she might have when we'd first met.

Elaina told me if I prayed, God would comfort me. I thought briefly, dehydrated and afraid, how foolish I was being. Her accomplice. Her enabler. But then, as I sat in the driver's seat, Elaina touched a bit of vomit on the side of my lips, licked the tip of her fingers. Sucked them.

"I can taste that he likes to test you. You made punishment too easy for him." Her voice was low. Then she gave me the kiss I was searching for. Long and probing and dominant. Her small hands pulling my face towards hers and when I wrapped my own around her wrists she pulled back.

"Let's drive to our new home now. Yeah baby?"

I nodded again.

Elaina rested her left hand on my knee, "I'm ready when you are."

I start slow.

Jesse, Jesse look at me.

I swell, the spirits in my ear, behind me.

Jesse what have we done Jesse look at me please.

I feel—

Jesse look at me, please look at me.

Jesse facing the door will not acknowledge me.

Has he not been tasked with seeing me all of the day?

I babble a bounty of words, maybe they are meaningless, but I continue them. Anything to secure the safety of his eyes in my direction. Each time he will not look I become more shrill, more dire. I pull off my shirt and underwire bra. I strip the polyester pads from my breasts, which have stopped leaking but are coated in rough red skin and spoiled milk.

Jesse look—

Jesse this is real. Look at all that's left.

I am on my knees and I crawl. I am as pathetic as

I can make myself and he will not look at me. Jesse is standing at the doorway, shoulders slumped like the weight of me is too much to bear, watching to where Claire has just followed her husband and the elders into the night.

I am laughing.

It is too funny.

We will be sucked back in.

There will be no way out.

I smell like the hospital and chemicals, and cheese, and somehow the woman at the bar's vodka and I smell of blood. With this invisible tether to the fetus and the blurry lines of the spirits I see a large carousel, and if I try to step off I will be crushed. But, I can see somewhere a man making a straight line towards a distance.

I remember when I was young, I was so small you could leash me with dental floss. With the thread of a coat. Just one knot around the neck and I would follow and do whatever was asked of me. Too small to even be noticed.

And now I must prove myself massive enough to Jesse to provide a gravitational pull, to be listened to, to be seen before he takes me with him.

Jesse.

When Jesse turns I see his anger quickly and I gasp and stumble to stand and turn to run.

Jesse is quicker and grips me hard around the upper arms and shoulders and turns me. He pushes me against the side of the bed and my knees buckle and I fall backwards. I squirm under his grip and he lies atop me. The weight forces the air of my body like a crushed bottle.

"I told you to shut up."

Jesse takes one hand around my jaw, turns me to look at his face while he pins me against the mattress. His chest against my naked breasts. Trapping me like this Jesse is hard. I can feel his erection.

"Shut up—" "Shut up and let me think."

I tell myself I am not crying anymore, that I stopped after the blessing. But there is water all over my face and my mouth is still moving. I tell myself I have stopped laughing, but it is not the spirit's hysterical cackle that fills the room.

Jesse's body is frantic pressing against mine, gripping me and I fight against him for a bit and then surrender to his greater strength.

"Baby, shut up. We found—" "She—"

Jesse presses against me like this a few minutes longer. He is not in control either. Jesse who is always in control. I think since this morning he has been corrupted, a crack put in him that has widened through the hours. The dream. The feminine taint.

His breathing begins to slow.

Jesse runs his hands along my hairline and scalp where I have been blessed with the oil. He kisses me here and moves his hands down along my wet cheeks. He puts his thumb in my mouth and I suck the tears and consecrated oil off the skin.

Jesse tells me, "Wider."

I do what he asks, but also he helps, pulling at the sides with one hand while he unbuttons his pants with the other. Jesse moves his body along mine on the bed and rests his hard cock against my cheeks, then lips. Then Jesse begins to fuck my mouth and throat. The tip of the shaft soft and round first against my teeth and tongue. I moan around him. I am still crying that quiet water along my cheeks and I can taste the salt of them mixed with the metal ridges of cock. He pushes himself past the barrier of my throat and I gag and choke, my nostrils sealed by Jesse's palm.

If only I could stop crying.

If only I could be either more, or less.

Jesse cums down my throat and the climax is a violent assertion which fills me up, my mouth up, so full my throat muscles flex and pulse and reject the material. I must turn my head, I still cannot sit up with him on top of me. I open my mouth and let some of the fluid onto the duvet. I spit. I lick my lips. I gasp.

Jesse slides down my body and buries his face in my stomach like he is ashamed. I still have more to say. I turn my head and I begin again to speak. He covers my mouth.

Jesse says, "You smell terrible."

I nod, but do not again try to make a sound so he will move his hand. The anger was a gift I realize. Now I am again my contrite and selfish tired being. I want to be anything that will keep him from again covering my nose.

Jesse speaks to my stomach. "This will be good—"
"Baby don't you want to be with them again?"

I do not know if Jesse means Elaina or Immanuel or
his wife. I do not know if he means our child. I think of
my sister.

I say, Jesse, would you like to see our baby?

He shakes his head like he is disappointed in me. I
climb off the bed even as he tries to grab at my wrists,
then ass and legs. I am still afraid but also I am slippery
and stubborn. I slide to the ice bucket and open it for
him to see.

"That is not a child." Jesse is sitting and his erection
is not fully faded. Is crawling back. A threat. I back
away.

"Jesus, can you—" "Baby. Please. Be a good girl?
Just for a night?"

Jesse's cock is still out. He is crying now too but he
strokes it a little, frowning as he massages the chalky
skin, looking at the locked door. Then he pushes it back
into his jeans. Pulls up the zipper.

I am still in my diaper and I feel it full of blood and
I have not buttoned my shirt. He looks away from me.
Jesse walks to the door.

I want to scream but instead I again begin to laugh.

The spirits have begun talking throughout this
scene of their own lives. They are telling me something
about blessings, about the now, about then. I am babbling again, shrill again over the noise of the spirits, or I
am trying to be shrill my voice is cracking I am weak.

Jesse does not look at me as he opens the door and the midwinter air shoots around my body, matter bereft of Elaina's light and heat. It slams closed behind him.

The latch clatters against the doorframe and jingles like a tiny tolling bell. I moan and my chin pulls to my chest, my sore throat hot. I open the bucket to look inside at what I am leaving behind.

I throw the lid of the bucket against the door and am suffering.

The spirits laugh at the suffering.

Elaina did not teach me how to pray. I remember being young and afraid or alone and pressing my body face first into the mattress and thinking dear God in heaven dear Jesus please bless me please bless me I can't do it, it hurts too much.

I ask Elaina, Who are we without our sins?

Elaina tells me, "Our essence. Our souls."

Elaina's irritation was sometimes a pleasure.

Shouldn't praying feel like sliding along Elaina's body?

Then I would do it more often.

Then all my sins would be resolved.

The room is still so cold.

Every moment to be remembered creates great caverns filled with moments that will remember them.

And I will be the person remembering in each of these moments, and so now I want nothing to happen. I have been made a coward by living I want nothing worth missing anymore. I press my body against the carpet and the spirits say, Baby why are you so stupid and I say God I want nothing worth missing. I say God I want nothing, please.

9 P.M.

I close my eyes praying and have a dream of a man on a
boat telling me that we respond to experiences we have
not yet had. I am enthusiasm. We are fishing. The sea
is black and the clouds approaching. Then retreating.
Then approaching. I tell the man who I think must be
Jesse, in a thick cable knit sweater—healthy and young
with red in his cheeks and hair—I tell this man I too
believe there is no linear time, and I begin to explain
my theories when the man quiets me. "Hush, baby."
And we eat fish we had not yet caught.

I open my eyes and the spirits are gawking. The drool
sticking to my cheeks, pools on the carpet. I pull myself
up to my forearms. I look down at my naked chest,
at the marks it has made on the ground. My diaper is
heavy with blood.

The spirits are tugging me towards them, like I am
more them than a stranger now.

I tell them, Stop it. He only leaves when he will be back.

I tell myself this even though it is a lie. Everything is a lie except that we all die. That we are not supposed to be on this land. That we do not understand our actions, and cannot comprehend their consequences. That we belong together, not alone. I sit on the floor holding the ice bucket to my naked chest and lean my head against the television stand. Stroking my cheek along the wood.

The spirits do not lie. The spirits who I thought were absent from the bar have followed me back from it. Must have been lurking outside. A group of women drinking tequila after a funeral. Two men discussing their shift at work. A man who says loudly, *Is anyone sitting here*, while touching himself through the longest pocket of his jeans. The spirits are always laughing. One, between hiccups of hilarity—*I cannot feel anything at all. Not a thing.*

I lie on the floor with the company of the spirits and the dead child in the ice bucket and take comfort in my three-faced devil. As if Jesse, Elaina, and I were all bound together by the torso. Spinning. Watching the trains go in circles around us coming closer.

I fall back into sleep.

10 P.M.

When I was finished telling the living god his stories
or singing his lullabies, I would place him in the crib.
Sometimes I felt the need to kneel before him, reach
my fingers through the bars in the furniture and touch
the hem of his garments, the pads of my fingers brushing along the ends of the sleeves covering his hands.
As though I had not just been coaxing small fistfuls of
air from the chest of the boy in case he burst with the
contained gas.

"Who has touched me?"

I turned to see Elaina, and resented her this dis-
missal of my closeness, even to a body once removed.

11 P.M.

There is air outside the room.

12 A.M.

I tell the spirits, There is air outside the room.

I wake suddenly, remembering the child is exposed.

I say aloud to myself, Hush, it is dead.

But still I crawl along the carpet, dragging my knees along the rough fibers. I fetch the lid to the ice bucket which I had thrown after Jesse.

I seal the baby inside.

I tell the spirits, It is safe.

I turn on the television and lie on the floor in front of it. The television is selling me knives. Knives for my husband for my dinner parties. I watch the knives slice lettuce and pears and rubber shoes and never a human hand. Never a lover's throat. I close my eyes.

A dream Elaina. Wherein, I'm sorry to embarrass myself and you further, but you tell me you love me. It shouldn't, but it still makes me cry.

In the dream you write me a letter demanding my company, so I take a train. In the dream the winter is over and the spring is stuffy on my limbs and in my lungs.

When the train stops, I walk along the platform full of early summer yellow cotton flowers, and I see I am back at the compound. I see a beautiful doe. It is an older doe, with pale golden fur unlike anything I have seen outside of myth. It bleats and a matching golden fawn hops across the grounds to stand beside it.

I walk towards the doe and fawn, my right palm open like I am safe.

The golden doe allows me to touch her ears and snout. Her fur is not bristled but soft and oiled. She nuzzles against me, the fawn leans against my legs. With my right hand I hold the fur of the doe in my fist, pulling, and with my left I pull a knife out of my pocket and run it along the front of its throat.

The fawn does not run but it should, instead bleating with grief, and I straddle it with my tall body and kill it next, stabbing it through the belly several times.

When I am finished I see you, Elaina.

You smile and nod.

All three of us watch as the doe's tongue lolls out of its mouth. The dust in the sunset glimmering in rays along its body. Its beauty already fading.

In the dream Elaina, you tell me that you love me.

Is this a dream, Elaina?

1 A.M.

My mother and sister are in a house but my mother
will not allow me back inside. The rain comes through
the roof and floods us and I say, please. Elaina, you will
not let me in either; you have been told by my mother
not to. You are leaving to go to dinner with a beautiful
woman, a mother of three. The beautiful woman's children are all eating strawberries. One of them is looking
at his strawberry very seriously, then begins to nibble
at the end. The child's lips turn blue and his face ash. I
throw water on him but it does not help. He claws his
throat and cheeks, his eyes popping. He dies.

Elaina, you tell the beautiful woman as she holds
the body and howls that if she had a little more
faith this would not be painful. This would not be a
problem, and, why can she not transcend these mortal
attachments?

2 A.M.

Jesse and I are touching each other in a stairwell. I am
about to let him kiss my neck, but then I tell him I have
to go home and take care of my son.

Tucked in my small house with my son, who is
Immanuel, an alarm goes off and I see a fire has begun
under my child's crib. The flames lick at the wood
which cradles him and I scream at the heat and pull the
child out by his arms, resting him against my chest then
hip as I run out the front of the door. I hold Immanuel
to me and Jesse is there and takes my son, who is suddenly not Immanuel, who is suddenly just a boy I do
not know. And Jesse walks away with the boy even as I
call out after them.

The firefighters begin speaking to me about rental
insurance and culpability.

As I am talking to them I see outside a caravan.
Jesse and the boy who sometimes is Immanuel and

sometimes is not, but also you, Elaina, also Martha and Georgette, also the elders, and also my stillborn girl, a goddess. A sun goddess like her brother. Wide with her father's ginger curls and she takes my hands and tells me it is not true she is not dead.

My daughter, "There is no end to life, baby."

I tell her not to call me that, but see she is older than me here.

I walk back to the burning house.

It is my grown and living daughter who ushers me inside to crisp.

I reach out for Jesse but find only the soft sounds of the television.

If you use ProActiv you will be beautiful.

Everything can change.

3 A.M.

After Immanuel was born, all was so happy in our
home. I remember that. There was never any contention. The power imbalances fell away. We ate again. We
drank. That same dark wine. That venison and those
chocolates. Even the lovemaking was easy and golden
again, all lit by firelight. Soft wet noises behind every
partition.

We followers were all in awe. Even the trees, which
were blooming, the green-tipped nibs of their branches
sparking out under the paternal gift of sunlight, sparkled at the idea of his presence. The tall canola more
golden, more yellow. Stalks which sang gorgeous
hymns in low winds. We would all lie in the sun with
the baby, over sheepskins and under wool. And we
were nourished.

And we thought something so pure and good
could never end, the baby would be drunk with milk
at Elaina's breasts. When Immanuel would change, so

much in even a day or two, and so suddenly be able to
wrap a fist around your finger.

My daughter must have little hands.

Elaina and I tripping through New York. Her
pulling at my jacket pushing me against walls, her hand
crawling up my skirt. Nipping at my ear and whispering, Do you like them to see? And once we passed a
church this way, the doors open and asking.

The two of us grew very solemn as we entered, but
still with an erotic charge that pulsed like an organ on
a table. A woman was crossing herself across the aisle
but otherwise there was no one to be seen. A soft light
filtered through colored glass and appeared before us
in dusty pillars. We held hands and we worshipped
together, Elaina bowing her head and letting my fingers
tremble along her spine.

I want to tell Jesse now, certainly the tree makes a
sound. How could you let her convince you otherwise?
How could you be so dense and easily manipulated into
believing nothing has meaning?

Immanuel and I were at the kitchen table. I had just given
him his evening bath. He had a cold and smelled like
Vicks. We were coloring a picture of Elaina in a castle. I
was adding a train to the scene with a small conductor
Manny on top of the engine, and Immanuel was smiling
to himself, filling the hat in with black crayon.

I smelled Elaina before I sensed her. Ethanol alcohol. Gasoline.

Elaina, in the same ratted white dress she'd been wearing for days, put her hands beneath Immanuel's arms and lifted him from his seat. She did not turn towards me once but Immanuel looked back over her shoulder as she began to walk out of the room.

I said, Elaina, what is happening?

But calmly, so as not to frighten Immanuel.

I said, Elaina, where are you going?

But she did not answer.

I followed her outside where the followers had built a small circle surrounding a wooden chair. I did not see Martha. I lost vision in my peripherals but felt each step Elaina made towards the chair and the slowness of it. The infinities capable of being held within a moment. I felt Jesse's hand on my back.

I pull at his hand to move forward but he is heavier than me and stupefied.

I trip and drop to my knees and he moves forward again.

I wake. I have been weeping in my sleep again. I have been doing this often. My wet face along the carpet.

I dig my fingers into the floor and scream against it until my throat hurts.

I calmly sit up. I stare at the ice bucket. I remove the lid.

I look for a while, then crawl to the table near the

bed, my breasts swinging and empty. I find in the nightstand a Bible and a matchbook. I take the matchbook. I
crawl back to the ice bucket.

I look inside.

I light a match.

I think to myself, This is no way to show love. And
also, It is dead.

A few times this cycles in my mind until the
match in my hand has burned itself all the way to my
fingertips.

I think, What will they do with the smell?

I light another match. Drop it.

The liner bag singes and curls around the small mass
of my daughter, but the small mound of tissue is wet
and cold and will not catch.

I watch the flame fizzle and go out. I close the lid on
the bucket.

Jesse and I are in stained petticoats. It is snowing and
he is too cold. He is sweet and calls out often for his
husband and child, who we buried the week before. I
kiss the tip of his nose and tell him to sleep.

I say, Baby, I truly understand—

Finally we understand each other.

Walking through a long icy canyon, I lead Jesse
where he needs to go. I am older than him in this dream
and have come to terms with my own losses. And I
have not been afraid of the end for some time.

This young and pretty Jesse with the frozen tears on

his cheeks asks, "Is the baby waiting for me in Zion?"
I tell Jesse, Your baby is dead.
I say, You have nothing but me.

4 A.M.

Jesse wakes me.

Jesse is leaning over my body and shaking me.

Jesse says, "We are meeting them tomorrow."

I say, I want whiskey.

Jesse sighs, annoyed. He does not think I am taking him seriously.

Jesse helps me off the ground and turns off the television and walks me to the shower and runs the water. He undresses me, helping me with the sticky tabs on the paper diaper, and I wince when it is removed, the dried blood pulls at my skin. He frowns a little as he binds it like a child's diaper, throws it in the trash. He then guides me under the steady stream of hot water and when I am submerged and wet he pulls hand soap from the sink and moves it along my body with the last washcloth. It stings the raw skin on my breasts.

I tell him, This is where the baby died.

But Jesse does not respond.

He moves the cloth along my shoulders. My stomach. He pulls my hair down my back. He washes my face with the tips of his fingers and stings my eyes, which were already running.

I ask Jesse if I can ask him a question.

I am careful. I whisper the I.

Jesse turns off the water and leads me out of the shower, wraps me in a towel. He helps me dry myself, dress in his boxers, his long flannel. He is trying to lead me to the bed and I whisper again, Jesse, can I ask you something?

He is careful too, he does not dismiss me.

He walks to the bathroom.

Jesse says, but not to me, "Can it wait?"

I have broken him but it cannot.

I say, Can I ask you now?

I hear Jesse pissing. Again the comforting drips. The clanging of the seat. He splashes his face.

Jesse leaves the bathroom. Jesse does not consent to my question, but he does not say no either.

I say, Jesse, what if there was a great storm.

Jesse, "Baby—" "Okay baby. What storm." "A storm like today?"

I say, No Jesse. Not like today.

I think of telling Jesse a story about a tornado, begin to, of Elaina's belief that she could not be touched by the weather ensconced in the city. That our brick and vaulted-ceilinged townhome would withstand any potential fate. That I knew her before him.

I change my mind.

I point at the scorched ice bucket.

I try to keep myself from becoming hysterical so Jesse will be more likely able to tolerate me.

I grip at his thighs and knees. I say, Jesse, what if the Earth is like Elaina, and she is leaving us? What if I do not have enough faith to watch it happen Jesse?

He shakes his head.

I say, Jesse, what if I do not have enough faith to have hope?

I say, But also, I, despite my lack of faith, feel full of meaning. I feel pregnant with suffering and still to believe in fate would be to decide to do nothing. More and more nothing. And your body Jesse, it can't hurt the way I hurt. And still I want to fight. I do not want to go quietly. I do not want to watch it again.

I am holding Jesse's knees between my legs and rocking. Pointing at the bucket still. Jesse tries to pull away, but I hold him still.

Jesse kisses my knuckles.

Jesse walks to the ice bucket and I flinch.

Jesse places it near me on the bed.

Jesse says, "You deserve some rest—"

Jesse says, "I'll have enough faith for both of us."

I whisper, Jesse you don't understand.

Jesse says, "I know about the storm." "Baby, if we do not sleep soon we will lose our minds." "We will—" "Oh please, baby. We will lose our minds."

Jesse lies on the bed with me and I am trapped

between him and the ice bucket. I begin to relax against his body. I listen to his breath.

Jesse strokes my forehead. He wants to show me he has been listening.

Jesse says, "We will talk with the elders in the morning. They will tell us what the prophet says about the coming storm."

I plead such pathetic little bleats.

Jesse's lids tremble and seal. He breathes so heavy that I am sure Elaina can hear it. That Immanuel will wake in the other room and cry out for us.

5 A.M.

Jesse, I worry this is the dream and whatever we've forgotten throughout the day might take us back if we close
our eyes.

6 A.M.

Elder Mond, as he approaches, is humming.

The song is pretty. Simple notes and careful full steps up, then slowly back down.

The tree yesterday morning who told me it was young now looks like it has itself sprung from Elaina's womb, C-section style, and has burrowed its way through her body and is shading us. It is swaying with the song. I hope one day it will be filled with fruit. That the fruit will drop. That the animals will eat.

The missionaries' song is an easy song to echo, and the spirits flock to my back like wings and trill and Jesse looks to me and I think for a brief moment sees that I am terrible and large.

But it is not an omen. The flicker fades and I tremble. I look for the sun but it is still too early and Jesse smiles. I smile. It is alright he sees the humor in it too. Of course there is no light yet. I take Jesse's hand

and it is a promise.

Mond's song is an echoing song and Jesse squeezes my hand in his, kisses the top of my head and taunts, "Sing it back then." The elders are closing in and the melody is so simple. It is inside me. I already know it. His echoing song.

I feel the spirits grow into huge grotesque clots, like jellyfish, corporeal as they flutter upwards, as if my faith had been the cage. I am now just bones and flesh. Jesse is standing in the door and the shadow he casts is a road and the room behind him an incandescent orange orb. But it emits no heat.

Elaina's revolution is past now. The latter days are upon us.

Acknowledgments

Thank you to Ben Fama and Francesca Kritikos for understanding and wanting this dark little book. Thank you to Francesca for making a home for *god* at Sarka, and all the work that has gone into its production. Thank you to Kit Ramsey for the perfect cover image. Thank you to Rick Rein for the tremendous support making god an audiobook.

Thank you to The Virginia Center for the Creative Arts and Tin House for supporting this project.

Thank you to my early readers. Thank you to the writers in my life who have influenced my thinking and work so significantly in and beyond this volume. Beth Nugent, Sara Levine, Taylor Croteau, Katie Bennett, Stephanie Cawley, Lauren Holguin, and the whole of Sunday Poetry.

In 2022 when I was in great pain with nowhere to

go, Dan Wilke gave me a home. He housed me while I completed much of this manuscript. I will never be able to correctly express the impact of that gift. To my dearest friends—Bess, Kurt, Sean, Joe, Jesse, Arden, Dan. I hope to list you all often and with continued love.

About the Author

Sam Heaps is a writer living in Philadelphia and teaching at Temple University. Their memoir *Proximity* was released through Clash Books in 2023. *The Living god* is their fiction debut.

9 798989 879849 18